CHRISTMAS CRISIS

A CHRISTIAN ROMANTIC SUSPENSE

FINNEGAN FIRST RESPONDERS

LAURA SCOTT

Elly Finnegan looked up in awe at the twinkling blue Christmas lights lining the parade route through downtown Milwaukee. This was her favorite time of year, and more so since she had planned a family reunion between her siblings and their Callahan cousins on Christmas Day. She'd found her grandmother's diary in the attic and couldn't wait to share what she'd learned with the rest of the family. The Callahans and Finnegans shared the same set of great-grandparents, but their respective grandmother siblings had lost touch with each other.

And now she knew why.

Since she was looking upward, she didn't notice the guy coming toward her until she'd bumped into him. Flustered, she smiled, and said, "Oh, excuse me."

His gaze sliced toward her. Her smile faded at the hard coldness reflected in his eyes. Elly genuinely loved people, and animals too, having made a habit of bringing strays home when she was younger, but there was something about this man that made the hairs on the back of her neck stand up in alarm. He wore a long dark coat that went to his knees, his hands tucked out of sight. Their gazes locked for a long, uncomfortable moment before he turned away and merged into the crowd without saying a word.

Evil. The word flashed in her mind, a weird sense of impending doom washing over her. But then she told herself not to be ridiculous. Tugging on her boxy navy-blue EMT uniform, she quickly made her way toward the ambulance. She and her EMT partner Derek were on duty for the Christmas parade. The assignment was a relief as the parade usually went off every year without a hitch. It wasn't likely she and Derek would have to deal with any actual injuries.

Okay, maybe she was getting better at dealing with her irrational aversion to blood, but there was still that moment of light-headedness she couldn't quite shake. Between that and the nausea that rolled through her abdomen, she'd barely managed to hold herself together the handful of times she'd been forced to deal with a bleeding injury.

Normally, she spent her days transferring patients from one location to the next. The ambulance company she worked for had contracts with most of the hospitals and nursing homes in the area. It wasn't exciting work by any stretch of the imagination, but she'd been deeply grateful for the uneventful transfers.

She really needed to find a way to push through this. The Finnegan family was all about being first responders, and she was determined to do her part. She'd already disappointed her oldest brother, Rhy, after failing first to become a cop, then again when she'd dropped out of the nursing program.

This career she'd chosen would work. It had to. There wasn't another option.

Crowds of people packed both sides of the street along

the parade route. She pushed through the throng, smiling at the memory of how her parents had brought her to the Christmas parade when she was young. Her parents had passed away eleven years ago now, and she still missed them. Although she was also grateful for her two oldest brothers, Rhy and Tarin, who'd stepped in to raise her after their tragic loss. As the youngest of nine siblings, she knew full well she was the main reason Rhy and Tarin had given up having a personal life to move back to the Finnegan homestead. Granted, the twins, Aiden and Alanna, had only been seventeen to her fourteen, but still. She had been the driving force behind their decision.

Thankfully, all her older siblings had found love in the past year. She was thrilled with the expansion of the Finnegan clan, including baby Colleen, the newest member of the family, born five weeks ago to Rhy and Devon. Joy's baby was due next April, and Kyleigh was pregnant now too. She had a feeling it wouldn't take long for the rest of the family to add to the Finnegan clan. Aiden and Shelby were getting married mid-January, so they had that momentous occasion to look forward to as well.

Glancing at her watch, she realized the parade was about to start. It would take about fifteen minutes or so for the parade to pass by her current location.

"There you are," Derek said. He was three years younger than her twenty-four, although her birthday was only a few weeks away. He'd asked her out, but she'd declined, not having any interest in him. Nice enough guy, but she'd been fighting a crush on Joe Kingsley—a cop who worked for her brother Rhy on the tactical team—for months now.

Not that Joe knew she existed. Well, other than being Rhy's baby sister. He all but patted her head as if she were ten every time they met. She shook off the depressing thought.

"This is going to be awesome," she said. Their position near the intersection was such that she'd have a great view of the parade.

"If we don't freeze to death," Derek muttered, stamping his feet and tucking his hands under his armpits. While she had to fight her aversion to blood while working, Derek had grown up in Arizona and hated, absolutely hated the cold weather.

Why he didn't just go back to Arizona was a mystery.

She caught a glimpse of a tall cop, and her heart gave a silly thump when she realized Joe was here too. In uniform and obviously working, the way she was. She stepped forward, but then forced herself to stop. She couldn't just rush over to say hi. Not while they were both on duty.

Especially since Joe had never hinted at having any sort of feelings toward her. She was nothing more than a pesky younger sister to him. Tolerated only because Rhy often put Joe in charge of the tactical unit. The sooner she accepted that fact, the better.

Christmas music rang out, indicating the parade had begun. She couldn't help grinning like a little kid as the marching band gave a rousing rendition of "Frosty the Snowman." She sang along, letting out a quick laugh.

The music grew louder as the marching band and the rest of the parade made their way down the street toward them. Elves tossed Christmas candy into the crowd, and a large float on a flatbed trailer had a pair of ice skaters dressed in cheerful red costumes doing twirls on the small patch of ice.

"Oh, that's so cool!" She was impressed the couple was able to spin and skate on a very small ice pond. When the male skater lifted the female over his head, she gasped and applauded along with the rest of the spectators.

Crack! Crack! It took a moment for her to realize the skaters were lying on the ice, bleeding.

Gunfire? Had that really been gunfire?

Screams reverberated around her. The marching band scattered. More bullets were fired, and people around her fell to the ground, not moving. Dear Lord Jesus, no!

There was an active shooter at the parade!

"Get down!" Derek tugged on her arm, trying to get her closer to the shelter of the ambulance. But when she saw Joe and several other cops rushing into danger, she surprised herself by breaking free of Derek's grip.

She grabbed the first aid kit and ran out to where she saw a young kid, barely eight years old, lying on the ground. Bile rushed into her throat and her head spun as she saw he'd been shot in the leg.

Don't faint! Don't faint! She knelt beside the child, but then as more gunfire rang out, she realized she couldn't stay there with him. Instead, she scooped him into her arms and ran, stumbling back to the ambulance.

"Here, take care of him!" She thrust the crying boy into Derek's arms. "Go inside the rig!"

Derek nodded and opened the back doors to carry the boy inside. She spun and ran back out into the street where the parade had abruptly stopped.

Her gaze landed on a cop sprawled on the ground on the other side of the street. *Joe? No, please, Lord, no!* Elly grabbed her abandoned first aid kit and darted through the screaming mass of people, nearly tripping over an abandoned tuba lying in the street in her haste to reach the fallen officer.

Not Joe, but a familiar face. She searched her memory

for his name as she avoided looking down at the massive pool of blood forming beneath him. Kyle. That's right, his name was Kyle.

"Elly?" He stared up at her, confusion in his eyes, as if he didn't understand what was going on. Frankly, she didn't either.

"I'm here. You're going to be okay." The edges of her vision blurred, and she had to tell herself again not to faint. *Not now! Please, Lord, not now!*

"El . . ." He tried to say something more, but then his eyes closed, and his body went limp.

Why was this happening? Her fingers fumbled on the first aid kit as she searched for gauze. As if the small amount she carried could stem the flow of blood running like a river across the frozen street. She swallowed hard, praying she wouldn't be sick. She pressed gauze to his groin wound, but instantly, it was soaked in blood. No use. It was no use!

"Elly!" It took a moment for her name to register. Dazed, she glanced up to see Joe making a beeline toward her, a look of panic etched on his features. Over his shoulder, she saw a man wearing a long dark coat standing above the others. He lifted a long automatic rifle.

"Down!" She screamed the word as loud as she could. Joe reacted instantly, as if she were Rhy shouting an order, and hit the ground as another crack of gunfire rang out. She watched in horror as Joe rolled over, lifted his own weapon, and returned fire.

The guy in the long coat ducked, then disappeared. She rose to her feet, stumbling toward Joe. "He's getting away!"

"Go back to the ambulance." Joe looked as if he wanted to stay with her, but he turned and ran toward the location the shooter had last been, talking into his radio as he went, no doubt putting the other officers in the area on alert to help him search. People were still screaming, some running away, others cradling injured loved ones close.

The entire scene was surreal and straight out of a horror flick. The amount of blood was paralyzing, but Elly forced herself to do her job.

The way Joe was.

Slightly calmer now that she knew the gunman had left the scene, she turned back to Kyle. When she couldn't feel a pulse, she forced herself to move on to the next victim. In times of a crisis, there was no time to waste on those who had no chance of survival. Not when there were so many other victims to assess and treat.

The next closest victim was a young woman being held by a man who was likely her husband. The woman was bleeding from an upper chest wound, but she still had a pulse. Despite being pale and in shock, the woman glanced at her. "Hurts."

"I know." Elly crouched beside them, using more gauze and pressing it against the exit wound. "Hold this," she instructed. The dazed man did as she instructed. "You're going to be okay. Let's get you up and over to the ambulance."

The man looked grateful for something constructive to do. She stood and helped him lift the injured woman. "Hang on to me, Lisa," he instructed.

"I don't understand," Lisa murmured. As if there was a way to make sense out of this horrible act of violence. "Why, Dan? Why?"

"I don't know." He pressed a kiss to her temple and half carried her across the street to the ambulance. There were other victims there now, too, having instinctively gone to the closest source of aid. Derek had the young boy inside, but he was now kneeling beside another victim. He glanced up as she approached.

He looked as if he wanted to say something, but then shook his head and went back to work. She completely understood. There was nothing else they could do but continue providing care until more help arrived.

The wail of police sirens was a welcome relief. Yet after she quickly assessed those with more minor injuries, she forced herself to head back out to the street.

There were several people up on the flatbed of the truck, tending to the two ice skaters. She had to swallow hard against another wave of nausea when she saw blood dripping off the edge and onto the street. Somehow, she managed to climb up.

"We need to get him to the hospital," a man was saying. "They need to get the Lifeline chopper out here ASAP."

"Are you a doctor or nurse?" Elly asked. The way they'd mentioned the Lifeline rescue helicopter made her think so.

"I'm a doctor," the young woman said. "He's a nurse. The female skater is dead, but the male is still alive."

"Okay, you stay with him. I'll keep searching for other victims." Elly told herself the injured skater was in good hands. Much better hands than hers, that was for sure.

She wanted to cry when she found another dead body, an elderly man who'd taken a bullet to his chest. But after that, she was grateful to find two more live victims.

After stabilizing their injuries as much as she was able to with her limited supplies, she helped them get over toward the ambulance. It seemed like the best place to keep the victims together.

As she worked, Elly couldn't stop thinking about Joe. Or the man in the long dark coat who had done this terrible thing.

The man she'd instinctively known was evil. Maybe even the devil himself.

JOE KINGSLEY HAD ONLY GOTTEN a glimpse of the shooter but tried to keep the brief image locked in his mind as he scoured the area searching for him. Using his radio, he'd alerted the other officers on duty, giving the brief description of short brown hair and a long dark coat. Steele Delaney was the closest to him, and they'd fanned out, scanning the area for their shooter. Yet he couldn't deny the perp could have easily dumped the coat and even the weapon by now. And there were still far too many people milling about, running chaotically around the scene of the crime making it difficult to quarter the area for a grid search.

It wasn't easy to leave Elly behind. His boss and her oldest brother, Rhy Finnegan, would expect him to find and apprehend the shooter while also keeping Elly safe.

Ironic that she was the one to save him by shouting at him to get down a split second before the shooter fired another three rounds. Narrowly missing him, and Elly.

They'd lost Kyle. After seeing the massive blood loss pooling beneath his fellow cop, he'd known the shooter must have hit an artery below the bullet-resistant vest they were all required to wear. The loss of a fellow tactical team member brought a fresh wave of anger. He'd been shocked and stunned when he'd heard the gunfire, then watched as the ice skaters went down on their small patch of ice.

These active shooter incidents were out of control. He'd never felt so helpless in his entire life.

They needed to find this guy! Most shooters killed themselves or kept firing until a cop took them out. But not this one. The fact that this shooter had sneaked away was outside the norm.

And he didn't like it. For all they knew, he'd escaped and was already planning his next shooting rampage. Maybe after he basked in the glow of his brutal success in taking out so many innocent victims. There was always an attention-seeking component to these events.

This one would be no different.

After a solid twenty minutes of searching, Joe, Steele, and Raelyn Lewis, the only three members of their team who had been assigned to the parade, had given up. He sent Steele and Raelyn out to scour for evidence, explaining his desire to check on Elly. Knowing Rhy would want that, too, the two cops had scattered to do what they could. He stood for a moment, considering what little he knew about their guy. The perp had seemed tall, but he had no way of knowing if the shooter had been standing on a chair or some other object while firing into the crowd.

On his way back to Elly, he stopped and provided aid to several victims who were thankfully not hurt too badly. Then he noticed dozens of cops swarming the area and knew additional help had arrived.

Now that the immediate threat was over, at least as far as he could tell, Joe was impatient to get back to Elly. He desperately needed to know she was safe.

There was a growing crowd around the ambulance carrying the logo that matched Elly's uniform. He pushed forward, raking his gaze over the group of people until he found Elly's auburn hair.

A wave of relief hit hard, yet he didn't stop until he'd reached her side. "Elly? Are you okay?"

"Joe." She turned and grasped his arm, leaning against

him for a moment before letting him go. "Did you find him?"

"Not yet." He winced at the disappointment in her gaze. "You're sure you're not hurt?"

She gave a slight nod, but her gaze skittered from his. She looked so pale that he feared she had been hit and didn't realize it. He raked his eyes over her, finding plenty of blood smears but nothing that appeared to be a recent injury.

"I saw him."

Her words were so soft with the chaos spewing around them that he wasn't sure he heard her correctly. He put his arm around her slim shoulders and pulled her close so he could speak into her ear. "What did you say?"

"I saw him." Her anguished gaze finally met his. "I literally bumped into him a few minutes before the parade started." She shook her head. "His cold, dead gaze made the hair on the back of my neck stand up."

An icy chill that had nothing to do with the winter weather washed over him. "You saw him up close?"

She nodded. "I didn't know he had a gun or that he intended to hurt anyone. If I had, I would have told you or another cop. The minute I saw him, though, I felt he was evil. And now—this—" She broke off, biting her lip.

"He is evil." Joe was still struggling with the idea that she had seen the shooter. "Elly, we're going to need you to work with a sketch artist so we can get an ID on this guy. Can you do that for us?"

"Yes, of course." Her voice lacked conviction, but she nodded slowly. "I'll do whatever is necessary for you to find this guy before he hurts anyone else."

"I know you will." He cared for Elly, far more than he should considering she was his boss's youngest sister. She was off-limits in a big way. Not that it was easy to ignore her when they were together. He was about to pull away when his gaze landed on her name tag pinned to her uniform.

Finnegan.

He could almost hear Rhy screaming in his ear. This was not good. He pulled Elly closer. "We need to call your brother."

"What?" She stared at him as if he'd suggested they take a walk on the moon. "Don't be ridiculous. We need to search the area for more victims."

"Elly, this guy might figure out who you are." He couldn't quell a flash of panic. "You're wearing a name tag. People in Milwaukee have heard a lot about the Finnegan family over the past twelve months. You couldn't have gotten any more press coverage than if you were Hollywood superstars."

She gaped, speechless, then shook her head. "You're exaggerating. The shooter probably isn't from this area. I'm sure he chose the parade because it was a good target . . ." Her voice hitched, then trailed off at the grim realization of how that twisted mind had purposefully come to the Christmas parade because it would be the best place to kill a bunch of innocent people.

He didn't have a chance to say anything more because more officers and medically trained first responders converged on the scene. He tried to call Rhy, but the call went through to voice mail. He left a quick message saying Elly was fine but that they were at the scene of the Christmas parade where a gunman had opened fire.

Elly continued to provide care to those who came to the ambulance, while other medical providers stepped up to help triage. The scene was still chaotic, yet he didn't dare let Elly out of his sight. For one thing, he hadn't been kidding about needing her to work with a sketch artist to create a composite of this perp.

But even more so, he wasn't putting anything past this guy. The destruction surrounding them proved what he was capable of. She had bumped into the shooter, thought of him as evil because of the coldness in his eyes.

While wearing a name tag that announced she was a Finnegan.

The thing that bothered him the most was that the shooter didn't fit the profile of the average active shooter. They were mostly young white men, angry at the world, bigots who purposefully took out people of color. Taking their anger out on those who couldn't fight back.

The gunman he'd glimpsed from afar was older, maybe in his midthirties. And he hadn't stuck around to become famous, like so many other active shooters had.

He'd slipped away.

His phone buzzed a few minutes later. He edged away from the crowd, still keeping his gaze on Elly as he answered Rhy's call.

"You're sure she's not hurt?" Rhy demanded.

"I promise she's not injured." But Joe knew Elly was hurt, deep inside. She was always smiling, full of fun and laughter, but today would likely have changed that for her.

And not for the better.

It made his heart ache, knowing she had lost her happy innocence.

"What happened?" Rhy was on vacation for the next two weeks over the holiday, or he would have been at the Christmas parade too. He shivered at the idea of Devon being here with their new baby.

He quickly filled Rhy in on the scant details he knew. Finally, he said, "The worst part is that Elly saw this guy up close. Apparently, she bumped into him. And, Rhy, she was wearing her uniform, complete with her name tag."

There was a long, tense silence on the other end of the line. Being on Rhy's team for the past five years, he knew very well that Finnegans didn't curse, but he could easily imagine Rhy wanting to. Maybe even saying the words in his head.

"Get her out of there, Kingsley. Bring her home."

"I will, but I'd like her to work with a sketch artist first." When Rhy didn't say anything, he added, "I'm sorry, but the shooter is still out there. We need to find him."

"Yes, we do. But do me a favor, stick to Elly like glue."

"I will." He was glad Rhy was on board with the plan he'd already intended to carry out anyway. "I'm taking her to the police station now."

"Thanks, Joe." Rhy's tone was softer now. "I know I can trust you to take care of my baby sister."

"You can." He lifted his gaze up to the heavens above, vowing to make good on that promise.

No matter what.

CHAPTER TWO

One by one, ambulances carted off injured victims. Elly and Derek had ended up assisting with triaging injuries, performing care to those with less serious wounds, leaving the worst for the volunteer doctor and nurses who had responded to the event. It was something her sister Alanna would have done if she hadn't been working. And Elly knew her sister would see many of these same victims once they were taken to Trinity Medical Center.

Nausea continued to swirl in her belly throughout the next hour. By now, it was more about the horrifying innocent lives that would be forever changed than it was about the blood. In some respects, she didn't really see the blood anymore.

She would not have chosen an incident of this magnitude to conquer her aversion to blood. Never. This type of thing happened elsewhere.

Not in Milwaukee, Wisconsin.

Although it had happened before. Not for the past ten years, but still. Logically, she understood no city was immune to domestic terrorism. But seeing the impact up close was the hardest thing she'd endured. Far worse than losing her parents eleven years ago.

Somehow, she managed to shove her personal feelings into a small box, working automatically as she cared for one victim and the next as if she were putting car parts together on an assembly line. Then suddenly there weren't any more victims. She stood, glancing around in confusion. Both sides of the street were empty now, no bystanders in sight.

The entire parade area had been cleared out. Probably by the police.

Exhausted, she stripped off her bloody gloves and tossed them into the garbage. She estimated that they'd gone through an entire box during the past two hours.

"Elly?" She turned to see Joe crossing toward her. "I've gotten permission to take you to the police station."

"I, uh, can't do that." She glanced over to where Derek stood near their rig. "I'm still on duty. We need to drive the ambulance back to the station."

"I'll take it back," Derek said. Despite his having three years of experience as an EMT, he looked a bit shell-shocked too.

She wanted to insist she was okay, but she wasn't. Images of the various injuries flashed in her mind. Memories that would haunt her for days to come.

"Please, Elly." Joe took her hand in his. "You agreed to work with the sketch artist, remember?"

"Yes. Of course." She hadn't remembered until he'd mentioned it. She looked down at her uniform, shivering at the blood stains. "I need to change first. I have clothes back at the station."

"That's fine." Joe didn't argue, which surprised her. "We'll follow your rig."

There was no reason she couldn't ride with Derek, but

she didn't say anything as Joe tugged her toward a police cruiser. He opened the door for her. She slid inside, buckled her seat belt, then closed her eyes and rested her head back.

Like clips from a movie, the images flashed through her mind. The sound of gunfire, the ice skaters going down, people screaming, more gunfire, the little boy she'd carried to the rig . . .

The shooter lifting his gun to aim at Joe.

No! She opened her eyes and reached over to touch Joe's arm. "He was going to shoot you."

"I know." Joe's smile was crooked. "You saved my life, Elly."

The statement hit hard. She'd never saved anyone's life. Certainly not during her EMT transfers from nursing homes to hospitals and back again.

"I'm sorry you had to go through that," Joe said when she didn't respond.

"It's worse for those who lost loved ones." She thought about the young man cradling his wife close. The dead female ice skater and her male partner who may or may not survive. "I've never seen anything like it."

"I know." Joe turned his hand palm upward. She took his hand and watched as his fingers curled around hers. "It was horrible."

"I'm glad you were there with me." She turned to look at him. He was following Derek back to the station. The ambulance company she and Derek worked for was small compared to some of the others. There were only three rigs, and the area inside the building wasn't much larger. They did respond to other calls, too, but that was mostly on night shifts and weekends when they took turns with other ambulance companies.

Elly had only been on a handful of other calls, facing

each one with deep trepidation. In hindsight, she'd been foolish to be so worried. Those calls had been nothing compared to what she'd experienced today.

Nothing.

"I spoke to Rhy." Joe's deep voice interrupted her thoughts. "He's worried about you."

"I'm fine." It was a lie, but she figured Joe knew that. "He should be focused on his new family."

"You're a part of his family," Joe said.

"I know." She sighed and turned to stare through the windshield. As the youngest of the nine Finnegan siblings, teasingly referred to as the oops baby, she'd stayed at the homestead far longer than she should have. If she'd have moved out sooner, then maybe Rhy wouldn't still see her as the fourteen-year-old who'd lost her parents. Her plan had been to search for an apartment after the holidays. In the meantime, it hadn't been a hardship to help Devon with baby Colleen.

Now she couldn't help wondering what her future held. She told herself the random shooting event wasn't likely to happen again in her lifetime but found it difficult to shake off the cloak of depression surrounding her.

She straightened when Joe followed the ambulance rig into the small parking lot of their building. Suddenly she couldn't wait to get out of her bloodstained uniform.

The minute Joe stopped the squad, she jumped out.

"Wait for me."

She ignored him, heading straight for the doorway. On off shifts and weekends, like today, there was a code to get inside. Without waiting for Joe or Derek, she entered the building and headed straight to her locker. She pulled out her jeans and green cable-knit sweater, then ducked into the bathroom to change.

If there had been a shower, she'd have used it. But there wasn't, so she had to make do. Despite her gloves, she had blood specks on her face and arms. She stripped to her bra and underwear, making sure there weren't other blood spots she might have missed. Stomach rolling with revulsion, she spent more time than necessary making sure she'd washed every inch of her exposed skin.

And when she was tempted to start over, repeating the process, she forced herself to stop. Sinking onto the commode, she buried her face in her hands.

This—she couldn't do this!

"Elly?" Joe rapped on the door. "Are you okay in there?"

She pulled herself together with an effort. Rising on shaky legs, she blotted the tears from her face and quickly pulled on her jeans and sweater. Then she removed the ponytail clip from her hair, letting the auburn strands hang loose. She still looked awful, but there wasn't anything she could do to improve her appearance. She opened the door and tried to smile. "I'm ready."

"Hey, you don't have to suffer through this alone." Joe wasn't fooled by her brave front. He pulled her into a hug, patting her back the way Rhy might have done. "After we get the sketch done, I'll take you home."

"Sounds good." She slipped from his arms and returned to the bathroom to pick up her discarded uniform. The one perk of the job was that the company laundered their uniforms if they were stained with blood. She stuffed the items into a basket, then returned to her locker for her coat.

"Take care, Elly," Derek said as she and Joe headed for the door.

"You too." She nodded at her colleague, then followed Joe outside. Oddly, the air seemed colder now, or maybe it was just a delayed reaction from the earlier adrenaline rush. Shivering, she slid into the police cruiser.

"He seems like a decent guy," Joe said as he put the car in reverse to back out of the parking spot. "Does Rhy like him?"

"Huh?" She glanced over in confusion. "Why would Rhy like him?"

"Oh, I thought maybe you two were dating."

"We're not." She looked away. The only guy she was interested in dating was the one sitting next to her. The one guy who would never ask her out. "He's too young."

"I see." Joe's tone was noncommittal.

She sensed he was trying to take her mind off the horror of the shooting. Normally, she'd have loved some private time with Joe. But not now. Not under these circumstances.

"The sketch artist is meeting us in fifteen minutes." Joe broke the strained silence. "Her name is Bethany Shear."

"Okay." She struggled to remain focused. "I'll do my best."

"She recognized your last name," Joe said. "Apparently, she worked with Brady and Grace back when Caleb was missing."

"You mean when he was kidnapped and basically rescued himself?" She had to smile at how Caleb had been brave enough to run away from the *mean man* as he'd called the kidnapper.

"Exactly." Joe smiled, and his craggy features became that much more attractive.

Talking about Caleb's bravery at the ripe old age of six helped give her the strength to pull herself together. This was hardly the time to fall apart. The danger was over. The sooner she worked with Bethany to identify the shooter, the sooner he would be arrested and tossed behind bars.

The entire city would sleep better when this guy was safely in police custody.

"My siblings have faced a lot of adversity over this past year." She glanced at him. "It seems the Finnegans are magnets for trouble."

"Funny, I would have said Finnegans were magnets for love the way everyone is getting married, engaged, and having kids." Joe shrugged. "There's trouble everywhere, Elly. It's how you manage it that counts."

Maybe he was right. She fell silent as he pulled into the district six Milwaukee Police Station. There were several districts for their large city, and she assumed this one had jurisdiction over the shooting incident. Rhy and his team primarily worked out of this district, while Alanna's fiancé, Reed Carmichael, worked out of district five.

Swallowing her nervousness, she climbed out of the squad and followed Joe inside. The bright lights made her squint until her eyes adjusted. The clock on the wall read nine thirty at night, making her realize she'd spent hours at the scene of the parade.

"You must be Elly." An older woman with dark hair threaded with gray came over to meet them. "I'm Bethany. Are you ready to get started?"

"Yes." She injected confidence into her tone, lacing her fingers together to hide the tremors. This sketch was important. Maybe the most important thing she'd ever do, other than warning Joe about the shooter. She could not mess it up.

"Great, this way." Bethany led her through a maze of cubicles. They stopped in one cubby where there were already two chairs set up, along with a sketchbook and colored pencils. "Please take a seat. I want you to be comfortable, okay?"

"Okay." She shrugged off her winter coat and took the chair across from the one where the colored pencils had been set out. "I'm ready."

"Perfect." Bethany flashed a reassuring smile as they began.

The process of capturing the face of the shooter was painstakingly slow. More so than Elly had anticipated. She hadn't remembered as many details as she'd hoped, but Bethany seemed to have tireless energy, making small tweaks along the way.

Describing the man's eyes were the easiest, although she couldn't really say for sure what color they were. She'd gone with dark brown or black, although it had been difficult to see the color clearly in the darkness.

"What about facial hair?" Bethany asked.

She shook her head, then hesitated. "Maybe a five o'clock shadow along his upper lip and jaw. But not a full beard."

"Great." Bethany beamed as if she'd gotten a difficult test question right. "Like this?"

Elly gasped when she saw the image. "Yes, that's him." A shiver snaked down her spine as if the evil man was standing before her once again. The likeness matched her memory better than she could have hoped.

And she found herself silently praying she would never come face-to-face with him ever again.

STAYING in the background so as not to distract Elly, Joe listened to her descriptions. Bethany was amazing, pulling out small details that Elly likely wouldn't have recalled on her own.

And when Bethany turned the sketch toward him and Elly, he knew they'd nailed it. The guy looked exactly like the shooter, matching the face he'd only glimpsed from afar.

"Good job, Elly. Bethany." He nodded as he stepped forward. "May I take that? We're going to scan it into the system and see if we can't get a facial recognition match."

"You can do that?" Elly asked.

"Sometimes." He didn't want to lie to her. "It doesn't always work with a sketch. Photographs are better."

"What about looking at street cameras?" Elly suggested. "That may help."

"That's being done. Unfortunately, that particular stretch of the road didn't have any cameras." He scowled, thinking that fact may have been the reason the shooter had targeted that portion of the parade route, rather than using the beginning or the end.

"It's yours," Bethany said as she tore the sketch free. He stepped over to take it from her. "I hope this helps."

"Me too," Elly said in a low voice.

"It will." He felt certain that once this BOLO went out, every single cop within the entire metro Milwaukee area would be on alert for this guy.

No one could hide forever.

The more concerning piece of this was what this guy might do in the meantime. He'd staked out the Christmas parade for a reason. Was there another target out there?

Most likely.

"Stay here, Elly. I'll be back soon." He took the sketch to the copy machine to get it scanned to his computer. From there, he sent the sketch to Rhy and to Rhy's boss, Assistant Chief Michaels.

Rhy must have been on his computer at home, despite

being on vacation over the holidays, because he got an instant reply. *Issue a BOLO ASAP.*

Joe typed his response. *Done.*

When that task was completed, Joe took a moment to head into the locker room to change out of his uniform. Officers were not allowed to wear their uniforms while off duty, which he now officially was. After dressing in black jeans, a dark-gray sweater, and his leather jacket, he clipped his gun holster to his belt and went back for Elly. Rather than chatting with Bethany, the way she usually did when meeting people, Elly stared off into the distance as if lost in thought. His heart squeezed painfully in his chest at how this may have changed the normally cheerful and carefree youngest Finnegan. And he wanted nothing more than to get his hands on the shooter.

"I'll be heading out now." Bethany rose to her feet. She'd packed her sketchbook and colored pencils into a large backpack that she slung over her shoulder. "It was nice meeting you, Elly."

"Yes, thanks for your help." Elly's smile didn't reach her eyes.

"We appreciate you coming in on a Saturday night," Joe added.

"Always for something this important," Bethany murmured. She nodded solemnly, then brushed past him to leave.

Elly stood, a frown puckering her brow. "I didn't realize you changed out of your uniform."

"I'm off duty." Technically not, since he planned to honor Rhy's request to stick to her like glue.

She nodded. "His sketch is going to be on the news tonight, isn't it?"

"Yes." He knew Assistant Chief Michaels would make

sure the press plastered this guy's face on every news station. "We'll find him, Elly. You'll see."

"I know, that's not my issue." She sighed. "I don't think I should go home to Rhy, Devon, and Colleen."

He grimaced, having already considered the ramifications of her returning to the homestead. "Rhy has a good security system."

"Colleen is barely five weeks old." Elly shook her head and crossed her arms over her chest. "I can't take the risk, Joe. And you know as well as I do you wouldn't put your family in harm's way either."

His sister and her husband lived in Green Bay, but Elly was right about how he'd never put them in danger. Yet Rhy was his boss and made it clear Joe was supposed to bring Elly to the homestead.

"I'm sure you'd like to grab a few things, though, right?" He figured he'd let her fight it out with Rhy. "No reason we can't make a quick stop."

"I don't like it," she said with a sigh. "I know we live in Brookland, far from the scene of the parade shooting, but if this guy does an internet search on my name, it wouldn't take him long to track down the location of our family home."

That was exactly what he was worried about. "He won't make a move right away, Elly. I'm fairly certain he's hiding out someplace, waiting for the heat to die down. Especially with his face plastered all over the news."

Indecision flashed across her features. He waited patiently, knowing she'd come around. When she finally nodded, he smiled.

"Thanks. My personal vehicle is out back." He took her arm, steering her deeper into the police precinct. "You might want to call Rhy, let him know we're on our way."

"Sure." Her half-hearted response concerned him.

He stopped at the back exit and turned to face her. "What can I do to make this easier for you?"

"Nothing." She waved a hand. "Reality is starting to sink in a bit, that's all."

"Elly." He held her gaze. "I know you better than you realize. There's something more."

She paused, then nodded. "If you must know, my measly six months of EMT experience did not prepare me for what happened tonight."

"What do you mean?" Her claim didn't make sense. EMTs must have some sort of trauma training.

"We had classroom training, but my job mainly consists of transferring nursing home residents to the hospital and back." She grimaced and ran her fingers through her auburn tresses. "I—blood makes me sick to my stomach."

He stared, trying to hide his shock. Wasn't seeing blood part of an EMT's job description? Then again, it sounded as if she hadn't been in many acute care situations. "Do you mind if I ask why you chose to become an EMT if you can't stand the sight of blood?"

"It sounds ridiculous when you say it out loud." She sighed and dropped her gaze to the floor. "I wanted to be a first responder like my older siblings. And I heard from a friend that EMTs weren't often called to the really bad medical emergencies, those go to paramedics like my brother Colin. I guess tonight has made me a real first responder. Instead of doing routine transfers, I ran out into the street to take care of a little boy who was hurt."

"Don't forget the way you saved my life." He could appreciate how growing up with the rest of the over-achieving Finnegans would have put some pressure on her. But to go into the medical field when you felt sick at seeing blood? That didn't make much sense. He wondered if Rhy knew, but then decided against saying anything to his boss.

"Yeah, that kinda surprised me too." She shook her head. "Guess I'm not useless after all."

"Never useless." He frowned, not liking that she'd even consider that.

Elly was a twenty-four-year-old adult. Five years younger than he was, but still old enough to make her own decisions. Even choosing a career that didn't suit her well.

Although she'd been amazing tonight, despite being thrust into a major blood bath.

If he could have spared her the experience, he would have. Rhy would say that this was God's plan. He wasn't sure he really believed that, but he wasn't about to question his boss. Or God for that matter.

"Call Rhy," he repeated, pushing through the exit. The cold blast of December air hit them in the face. He held the door for her, then gestured to the SUV in the corner. "That one is mine."

"I remember." Elly hunched her shoulders against the wind and headed toward it. He walked beside her, scanning the area.

When they were settled in the SUV, he started the engine, then blasted the heat. "You have a seat warmer too." He touched the control.

"The next car I get is going to have seat warmers." She leaned forward to set the level to high. "Now this is luxury."

He chuckled, appreciating her light tone as he backed out of the parking lot. The ride to Brookland wouldn't take too long at this hour, even though it was a Saturday night. He decided to take the interstate, knowing Rhy would be waiting up for them, rather than getting some badly needed sleep.

As if reading his mind, Elly pulled out her phone. "Hey, Rhy, don't worry, I'm fine. Joe is bringing me home."

He couldn't hear the other side of the conversation but imagined Rhy would press for more information on what had transpired.

"I'll give you more information when we get there. See you soon. Give Devon and Colleen a hug and a kiss for me." She lowered her phone. "Rhy is waiting up for us."

"I figured." Rhy was very protective of his family. It wouldn't have mattered if the hour was two in the morning, he knew Rhy would have stayed up.

The tactical team liked and respected their captain. But they were also a bit in awe of him. It was rare that Rhy let his temper fly, but when he did? Watch out.

He had no intention of being on the receiving end of Rhy's wrath.

Fifteen minutes later, he exited the freeway and headed toward Brookland. His one-bedroom apartment overlooked the Milwaukee River. He normally liked being closer to the lakefront, but there was something to be said for the peaceful serenity of the Brookland suburb.

"I hope the shooter is caught soon," Elly said as he slowed the SUV. Rather than pulling straight in, he backed up into the driveway. Better to keep his eyes on the road just in case.

The Finnegan homestead was a large two-story redbrick home with white trim and black shutters. The place had six bedrooms, which sounded like a lot until you considered what it was like when all eleven of the Finnegan family members had lived there.

"We'll get him." He offered a reassuring smile. "Guys who do this type of thing are loners, outcasts. I doubt he has friends willing to hide him from the police."

She nodded thoughtfully and reached for the door handle. "If he has family, I hope they turn him in."

"I'm sure they will. Hold on, I'll walk you up." He pushed open his door when she surprised him by leaning over to kiss his cheek.

At the same moment, a gunshot reverberated through the night.

CHAPTER THREE

Elly instantly ducked her head, wave after wave of panic washing over her at the sound of gunfire. Instantly, she was back at the side of the road watching the ice skaters as they collapsed in a crumpled heap on the flatbed trailer. Then the little boy, lying in the street crying and bleeding.

No! No! No!

"Stay down!" Joe started the SUV, shifted into gear, and hit the gas. The vehicle shot out of the driveway.

She struggled to pull herself out of the flashback and into the present. They weren't at the parade anymore. They were at her home. "Wait!" She tried to lift her head, but he ruthlessly held it down. "What about Rhy, Devon, and Colleen?"

"I'm sure Rhy heard the gunfire." Joe's voice was tense with anger. "That slug barely missed you. Came through the windshield."

It had? She didn't feel any cold air, but that could be because her heart was thudding so fast it was as if she were running a marathon. Not that she'd ever done such a thing.

Her mind whirled, images of the man she'd sketched sitting somewhere outside her family home, just waiting for her to show up.

"If you hadn't leaned over at that moment . . ." He didn't continue. Her cheeks burned as she realized her attempt to kiss him had saved her life.

Now they were even. Yet the grim realization didn't make her feel any better.

Seconds ticked by as Joe navigated through the neighborhood. Sitting hunched over the center console, with her face practically in his lap, was making her feel dizzy. She needed to be able to see where they were going. Especially as she kept lurching from side to side with his unexpected movements.

Finally, she pushed at his arm. "I feel sick."

Instantly, he let her go. She sat up but hunched down in the seat. She drew in a ragged breath, staring at the bullet hole in the windshield that was at the same level as her face. Her face! She couldn't tear her gaze away. A fresh wave of nausea hit hard as she understood just how close she'd come to being murdered in her own front yard.

"I don't understand." She had to force herself to turn away. "Did the parade shooter do this?"

"Yeah, unless you have other enemies I don't know about." Joe's phone rang. The name on the dashboard screen simply said *Captain*. Joe punched the talk button. "Elly is okay. She's not hurt."

"What happened?" Rhy's tone was sharp.

"I have reason to believe the parade shooter has come after Elly." Joe's blunt assessment made her shiver. "She saw him up close while wearing her uniform with her name tag on. Then she worked with a sketch artist to make a decent likeness of him. I have to assume he found out where the Finnegan family home was located."

"These types of shooters normally crave media attention. They want to go down in history," Rhy said. "They don't keep coming after someone who witnessed them taking random shots at strangers. Why is this guy different?"

"I don't know." Joe sounded frustrated. Elly couldn't blame him. She couldn't begin to comprehend why this was happening.

She found her voice. "I'm fine, Rhy, but I'm worried about Devon and Colleen. Maybe you should get your family out of there."

"Or I can get Steele, Raelyn, or one of the other teammates to come sit on your house for the rest of the night," Joe offered. "I—don't know if you heard, but we lost Kyle."

There was a long silence as her brother digested this. Elly knew Rhy considered his team to be like members of the family. Losing one of their own would hit hard.

Joe continued to make several turns, winding through the Brookland neighborhood. Finally, Rhy said, "I'm sorry to hear we lost Kyle. And that only makes me more determined to figure out what's going on. According to the news, there were ten people killed and at least two dozen injured."

"That sounds about right." Joe glanced at her, then added, "Elly was amazing. She ran out into the street to rescue a young boy. She also saved my life."

"And now Joe has returned the favor." For some odd reason, she didn't like the way he seemed fixated on those brief moments when she'd watched the shooter take aim at Joe and shouted a warning. Anyone would have done the same thing. She'd reacted without thinking, hardly heroic.

"I'm sorry, Rhy. We never should have come to the homestead."

"Don't be ridiculous, this is your home." Rhy sighed heavily. "Joe, please take Elly someplace safe. I'll get in touch with the team to see who's available to sit out here tonight. I don't like wasting resources, though. Every cop on the street should be out searching for this guy."

"Alert the Brookland PD," Joe suggested. "I'm sure the shooter is long gone, but maybe they can find something, evidence that we can use to find him."

"Did he leave anything behind at the parade?" Rhy asked.

"Not that I'm aware of. I had Raelyn and Steele out looking for signs of shell casings or anything else that might be evidence, but there were too many people and innocent victims. I believe they found some casings, but not likely all of them. I planned on having them search again tomorrow morning."

"I'll call Brookland, then touch base with Steele." There was a slight pause before Rhy added, "Please keep Elly safe."

She didn't like hearing the worry in her brother's tone. "I'll be fine, Rhy. I will feel better knowing Devon and Colleen are safe too."

"I'll head to the American Lodge," Joe spoke up. "I know it's only a week before Christmas, but hopefully Gary will have a couple of rooms available."

"Sounds good. If not, let me know and we can rent something." The sound of a baby crying came through the speakers. "I have to go. Keep me updated."

"Will do." Joe punched the end call button.

She drew in a deep breath and let it out slowly. The

bullet hole stared at her, but she decided to look on the bright side. God had been watching out for her. She was alive and so was Joe. All she could ask was for her family to be safe.

"The American Lodge, huh?" She tried to smile even though her heart was heavy. "I've heard so much about the place but have never been there."

Joe nodded, glancing at her. "I know Rhy and several of your other siblings have used it before. Gary Campbell, the owner, is a former firefighter and is happy to give special rates to cops and firefighters."

"Sounds like it's finally my turn to check it out." She strove to keep her tone light, despite the threat of danger. The sketch of the shooter flashed in her mind. "Do you think he saw his face on the news already?"

"That's a good question." Joe looked thoughtful. "It didn't take us that long to get from downtown Milwaukee to your place. Even if the sketch went out to the media in record time, the news outlets would have had to fit the breaking news story into their schedule. It seems unlikely that this guy could have seen a news story featuring his face prior to the gunfire at the house. Not if he was stationed outside the homestead, waiting for us to show."

A shiver rippled over her skin. The very thought of this guy sitting somewhere close to her family home with a gun was terrifying. "I hope your teammates agree to watch over Devon and Colleen."

"They will." Joe spoke with confidence. "Especially after the way we lost Kyle Malaki to this guy."

She nodded. Kyle had been a nice guy. Everyone that she'd interacted with on Rhy's team was just as honorable. She'd met Kyle on several occasions, and it made her heart hurt to know he'd been killed by an evil man with no conscience.

Yet deep down, she was selfishly relieved Joe hadn't been hurt.

When she spied the American Lodge, she had to admit she had been expecting something more after hearing so much about the place. The two-story white building was nice enough but not large. From what she could tell, there were twenty-four rooms, twelve on each floor, all facing the parking lot.

"Gary keeps the place clean," Joe said as if reading her thoughts. He pulled into the parking lot and stationed the SUV directly in front of the main lobby doorway. "Stay where you are, I'll come around to open your door."

She sighed and nodded. Joe was going above and beyond the call of duty because she was Rhy's little sister. The youngest Finnegan. Rhy's team would walk barefoot over fire for him.

Protesting would be useless.

Besides, the small bullet hole in the windshield was difficult to ignore. A constant reminder of the fact that the shooter wanted her dead.

Just because she'd bumped into him?

Probably. After all, he'd ruthlessly gunned down dozens of innocent people enjoying a holiday parade.

Joe opened her door. Sliding from the vehicle, she forced herself to stand on shaky knees. She needed to pull herself together. The danger was over. She waited as he closed the car door, then took her elbow to escort her inside.

A man in his midfifties was seated behind the counter. He straightened, then grinned. "Well, if it isn't Joe Kingsley, Rhy Finnegan's right-hand man."

"Hey, Gary." Joe stepped up to the desk offering a grin.

"This is Elly Finnegan. I'm hoping you have a pair of rooms for us to use for tonight."

"It's nice to meet you, Elly." Gary extended his hand, and she shook it. So did Joe. "Of course, I have two connecting rooms, but they're on the second floor."

She caught the grimace that flashed over Joe's features. Then he nodded and handed over his credit card. "Okay, that will have to do."

Gary nodded as he swiped the card. "I understand it's not optimal to be on the second floor, but I have security cameras now, so that should help."

"That is reassuring." Joe took the two room keys and credit card Gary slid across the desktop. "Thanks."

"The Finnegan family has been in danger more than anyone else," Gary said thoughtfully. "Well, the Callahans had their run, too, a few years back."

"The Callahans are second cousins to the Finnegans," Elly said. "It's been great getting to know them."

"That explains why both families have similar blood running through their veins," Gary joked. Then he sobered. "I'll keep an eye on the security cameras tonight."

"Take my phone number." Joe rattled it off as Gary punched the information into his cell phone. "Call me if you see anything remotely suspicious."

"Will do." Gary stepped back from the desk. "Sleep well."

Joe nodded and once again took her elbow. She did her best to ignore the warmth of his fingers radiating through her down coat. He steered her toward the car, opening the door for her.

"I can walk." She scowled.

"I'm going to park in the rear of the building, closest to

the outside staircase." He gave her a gentle nudge. "Trust me, okay?"

"I do." She managed a smile as she slid into the passenger seat. Joe Kingsley would protect her with his life, not because of her personally, but because of his dedication to Rhy and the rest of the tactical team.

And that would have to be good enough.

DESPITE BEING STUCK on the second floor, Joe was thankful to have connecting rooms. Sharing a room with Elly would have wreaked havoc on his concentration. As if it wasn't already hard enough not to notice how beautiful she was, and how strong.

The bullet had barely missed her, but Elly had bravely soldiered on, reassuring her oldest brother she was fine.

He wasn't fine. Not after that near miss.

They'd already lost Kyle. He could not, would not lose Elly. As he pulled around the American Lodge, he tried to come up with an escape plan. He parked the SUV a few feet from the stairs.

It wasn't ideal, but he was banking on Gary's security cameras to give them a fair warning of a potential threat.

He pushed out of the driver's side, then went around to help Elly squeeze out between the door and the building. "You must think I'm smaller than I am," she groused.

She was perfect, but he managed to hold back from saying so. "Sorry. If we need to leave in a hurry, I want you to crawl into the back behind the driver's seat."

"Um, okay." She shot him a sidelong glance. "You think we'll have to leave in the middle of the night?"

"I'm sure you know Rhy expects us to be prepared for the worst." He took her elbow.

"Yeah." She didn't say anything more as they rounded the corner of the building and took the stairs to the second floor. Thankfully, their two connecting rooms were at the top of the stairs. At least they had easy access off the second-floor landing.

Better than jumping over the railing.

He used one of the keys to unlock the first door, the one at the top of the stairs. Pushing the door open, he handed Elly the key. "This is your room. Please open the connecting door on your side, okay?"

"Sure." She took the key and crossed the threshold. He closed her door tight, then moved to the next room.

Minutes later, he had his connecting door unlocked and opened. He listened as Elly moved around, then finally opened her side.

"So now what?" Elly gestured for him to come into her room. She'd tossed her winter coat onto the foot of the bed. "What can we do to find this guy?"

"*We* aren't going to do anything." The words spilled out before he could stop them. "This is a job for the police, and maybe even the FBI."

"Good point." Elly nodded. "I'll call Brady."

"Whoa, hold on." He held up his hand. "Seriously, Elly, you need to let the police handle this. You did your part by helping to create the sketch. We can take it from here."

"I'm not an idiot." She scowled, and there was no reason that should have made her look cute. "I can help."

He stifled a sigh. It wasn't that he didn't think she was smart or capable, but she was an EMT who didn't like blood. She was as far away from being a cop as he was from being the king of England.

Yet there was no point in arguing. "We'll see what can be done in the morning. For now, you should try to get some sleep."

She crossed her arms over her chest. "Is that what you're doing? Getting some sleep?"

It was tempting to lie, but he couldn't do it. For one thing, Rhy hated lies, a trait that went way back to when his fiancée had cheated on him. That was well before his boss had met Devon, and in the end, things had worked out exactly as they were meant to. Secondly, he respected Elly and needed her to keep trusting him.

"No. But that's only because I have a few calls to make." He spread his hands wide. "Honestly, Elly, there isn't anything for you to do. Not tonight."

She stared at him for a long moment, suspicion clouding her dark-brown gaze. Then she turned away. "Fine. I'll watch TV, see what the news is saying about this guy."

"No, please." He took a step toward her. "There's no reason for you to watch the news. You saw the guy. You were there to witness the horror. I don't want you to relive that."

She grimaced, picked up the remote, and turned on the television. He wondered if she was doing it on purpose to drive him crazy. She glanced over her shoulder, her gaze weary. "The images are already seared into my memory, Joe. The minute I heard the gunshot at my family home, I was back in the thick of the terror. There's nothing I can do to stop reliving it. Other than maybe helping to find this guy."

He hated, *hated* that she would suffer nightmares over this. Yet she was right in that there was nothing either of them could do to stop it. He'd suffered his share of PTSD from horrifying calls he and the team had responded to. On particularly brutal slaying had stuck with him for a long time.

The Christmas parade shooting would likely be the same for Elly. And honestly, for him too.

"I need you to keep your side of the connecting door open at least an inch or so." He gestured to the opening between their rooms. "I won't invade your privacy, but I need easy access if I hear from Gary."

"Understood." She turned her attention to the television. He followed her gaze, catching the breaking news headline as the sketch Elly had helped create flashed on the screen.

"Police are asking for the public's help in identifying this man," the somber news anchor said. "Please call the tip line if you know this man's name, where he lives, or how he can be found. He is considered armed and dangerous, so the police are asking that anyone who knows him stay away. Do not approach or attempt to apprehend him on your own. If you see him, call 911 and report the location." The news anchor went on to repeat the phone number while the sketch of the gunman remained on the screen.

"Well, that should shake something loose," Elly said in a low voice.

"Yeah." He hoped that was true. He needed to believe his cop colleagues would have him in custody by tomorrow morning.

Bringing an end to the danger surrounding Elly.

He turned away, raking his hand through his hair. Crossing into his room, he glanced around. After removing his leather jacket, he decided to sleep with his clothes on in case they needed to go on the run again.

They were safe here. This random shooter would not

have any way of tracking him and Elly to the American Lodge motel.

So why couldn't he relax? He paced the length of the room, his mind going back over the shooting incident. Then he abruptly stopped.

What if the shooting wasn't random?

He quickly crossed the room to listen at the connecting doors. Hearing the TV, he pushed her side open a bit. "Elly? Are you decent?"

"Yes, I'm dressed." She lowered the sound on the TV.

He edged into the room. She was propped up against the headboard, pillows piled behind her back. "I have a few questions. How much time passed between the time you saw this guy and he started shooting?"

She frowned. "I bumped into him roughly fifteen minutes before the parade started. The marching band was playing 'Frosty the Snowman,' but they didn't come into view right away. Maybe ten minutes passed before they made it to our section of the street. I was watching the ice skaters. One minute they were spinning around the small patch of ice, the next they were lying on the truck bed covered in blood."

He moved closer, then dropped down onto the edge of the bed. "Do you think he shot the ice skaters first?"

Her brow furrowed as she searched her memory. "Yes. I think the ice skaters were his first victims. I didn't realize what happened, I was so shocked. But then the gunfire continued, and people began to scream and cry out as they fell to the ground."

The ice skaters. He pulled out his phone and searched for their names. They were local, he knew that much. And they'd been winning skating events over the past few months, which had garnered media attention.

"Gabrielle St. John and Henry Watkins." He lifted his gaze to hers. "The woman died at the scene, right? Gabrielle?"

"Yes." Her eyes widened. "You think the shooter killed her on purpose?"

"It's possible." It didn't make sense that the gunman would kill Gabrielle and injure Henry along with so many others.

Unless he wanted them to believe the event was a random shooting, much like the other shooting events that took place across the country.

"That's sick," Elly whispered.

"Yeah." Or creepily smart. He wanted to call Rhy but settled for sending an email to him and Assistant Chief Michaels instead. Rhy was on vacation, taking well deserved time off to care for his wife and newborn baby daughter. The information may or may not be as helpful as he'd hoped. But maybe once they got an ID on the guy, they'd learn his true motive. "Thanks, I appreciate the insight."

She reached out to touch his shoulder. "I want to help, Joe. Please. I keep thinking back to the moment I bumped into him. How I instantly got a bad vibe from him. Maybe if I'd have said something, this wouldn't have happened."

"Even if you had mentioned brief interaction to me, there would have been nothing I could do," he hastened to reassure her. "There wouldn't have been probable cause to search him for a weapon. Not unless he'd done something to break the law."

"I guess." Her arm dropped back to her side. He forced himself to stand, to stay out of reach. "But I still want to help."

He nodded. "We should know more tomorrow. Good night."

"Good night." She lifted the remote and turned the TV off.

Safe in his own room, far from temptation, he stretched out on the bed, pondering the possibility of Gabrielle being the actual target. But even that didn't explain why the shooter had come after Elly. If he wanted this to be viewed as a random shooting event, targeting a witness only brought more scrutiny to the rampage.

He checked his phone, but there was no response yet from Rhy or Michaels.

Setting the device near his pillow so that he would hear if Gary called, he stared up at the ceiling.

He hadn't intended to fall asleep. Not after promising Rhy he'd watch over Elly. But somehow, he did.

He woke slowly, blinking in the darkness. There was nothing but silence surrounding him. A noise hadn't woken him. Reaching for his phone, he stared at the screen. A wave of relief hit hard when there were no missed calls from Gary.

Swinging into a sitting position, he straightened his MPD sweatshirt. Sleeping fully dressed was far from comfortable.

He stood and stretched. Before he took more than two steps, the loud crack of gunfire followed by shattering glass had him diving toward the connecting door.

"Elly!" Her name was a hoarse croak as he pushed her door open and crawled through the opening. Raking his gaze over the bed, he quickly noted she wasn't there.

Where was she?

"Elly!" he shouted now, panicked as he continued crawling through the room, braced for the next round of gunfire. It came barely two seconds later. The bullet hit the center of the mattress. Briefly, he understood the shooter must be higher than their second-floor rooms.

"Joe! I'm in the bathroom!"

"Get into the bathtub!" He grabbed his phone and called 911 to report the gunfire. They were pinned in the room like ducks sitting in a pond. And he grimly realized they could be injured or worse before the police could get there.

CHAPTER FOUR

Elly huddled on the floor in front of the vanity, shaking at the sound of gunfire. In her mind's eye, she saw the skaters falling again, awash in blood. It was only when she heard another round of gunfire that she realized she needed to move.

She crawled to the bathtub, lifting herself up just enough to make it over the rim and down inside. She turned so that she was lying face down. Every muscle in her body trembled with fear. Images of dead and injured people flashed through her mind. It was difficult to dissect what had happened earlier from what was going on now.

Partially because she'd awoken crying and drenched in sweat from a terrible nightmare. One in which the shooter had aimed and fired round after round into Joe's body. Nausea swirled in her stomach, and she had to fight the urge to throw up. She'd pushed the sweaty blankets aside and had come here to the bathroom to wash up. Until the sound of gunfire had sent her diving down to the floor.

And back in time.

"Elly? Are you with me?" She could hear Joe's voice

getting closer and easily imagined him making his way across the motel room to find her.

"Yes." Her voice was little more than a croak.

Another barrage of gunfire exploded through the night. A bullet ripped through the bathroom wall, shattering the mirror above the sink. She instinctively ducked lower, covering the back of her head with her hands.

Please, Lord, make it stop!

"Elly." Joe's voice had her glancing up. He was in the bathroom, crawling over the edge of the porcelain tub. It was too small for the two of them. She tried to scoot over to make room for him, but he draped his body across hers, propping himself on his elbows and knees. "Stay down, okay? Help is on the way."

"A-are you hurt?" Her teeth were chattering although she didn't feel cold. It took her a minute to realize she was in shock. A phenomenon she'd learned about in her EMT training program but had never experienced firsthand.

There was a lot she'd learned but hadn't put into practice. Until now.

"I'm fine." He shifted his weight to move his hand over her arm, then down her back. "No injuries?"

"Not that I know of." She pushed the words through her tight throat. "How did he find us at the motel?"

"I don't know." Joe's tone was grim. "The only possibility is that he got my license plate number earlier."

That didn't make any sense. Granted, the shooter could have gotten the number from when they were out in front of the homestead, but how did some loner with an assault rifle trace the license to Joe? She wasn't a cop but had learned enough from her older siblings to know that wasn't an easy task for the average citizen. "Who is this guy?"

"That's a good question. Unfortunately, I don't have an answer. Not yet."

She didn't know what to say. She wasn't naive, she knew police work took time. But it seemed unbelievable that this guy had managed to stay under the radar long enough to make two more attempts to get to her. Escaping three times, unless the officers who came managed to find him.

Why? That was the confounding question.

Joe shifted his weight. "Sorry, I hope I'm not crushing you."

"It's fine." She could have told him she'd wanted nothing more than to be held in his arms, but not like this. Not hiding in a motel room bathtub from an evil man intent on killing them.

The sound of gunfire abruptly stopped, leaving an eerie silence behind. She wanted to believe that meant the shooter was gone, but knew better than to make assumptions.

Finally, the wail of police sirens indicated help was on the way. She told herself they were safe now. That the shooter was long gone. Yet the thought didn't bring much relief. She couldn't seem to stop shaking. She willed herself to calm down, but that was about as effective as spitting in the wind.

As if sensing her distress, Joe tightened his arms around her. "I'm here, Elly." His low husky voice helped bring her stress level down a notch.

"Joe! Are you okay?" a deep male voice called out.

"In the bathroom, Steele." Joe abruptly lifted himself up and off her. It was all she could do not to grab onto him to keep him close.

"This place is shot up pretty bad," Steele said. "No injuries here?"

"We're good. Better than the motel room." Joe stood and stepped out of the tub. "I want everyone out there searching the surrounding area for this guy. We need to find him. And I also want you to check with Gary on his security cameras. This guy shouldn't have gotten this close without alerting us."

"Will do. After I get you both out of here."

Elly glanced up to see a broad-shouldered cop standing there in full combat gear. She remembered Joe called him Steele. She wasn't sure if that was a first or last name. He gave her a solemn nod. "Ms. Elly. Are you hurt?"

"No." She sat up in the tub but couldn't stand. Not yet. Drawing in a deep breath, she abruptly realized why Steele had gotten there so quickly. "You were standing guard at the homestead, weren't you?"

"Yes." Steele gave a slight nod. "Your family is fine. As soon as I heard the report of gunfire, I knew you and Joe had been targeted."

"But why?" She couldn't wrap her mind around it.

"We'll find out more once we grab this guy." Steele turned to Joe. "I have Brock and Raelyn outside searching. I'll head out too."

"I'm coming with you." Joe stepped forward, then paused to look back at her. "Hold on, maybe we should get Elly outside and into a squad."

"Good idea," Steele agreed. "Keep her close."

Since both men were looking at her expectantly, she forced a nod. "Okay."

Joe stepped forward and offered his hand. Gathering her strength, she took it and stood, hoping her legs wouldn't collapse. She carefully stepped out of the bathtub, avoiding the shards from the broken mirror that littered the floor.

"You need shoes." Joe frowned. "Where are they?"

"Next to the bed." She took the few steps to reach the bathroom door. Steele left, returning a few seconds later with her running shoes in his hand. She reached for them. "Thanks."

He nodded, then stepped back, casting a glance around the room. Leaning on Joe for strength, she slipped the shoes on. Moving into the main room, she abruptly stopped when faced with the damage.

The room looked as if it had been attacked by a band of guerrilla fighters rather than one lone gunman. There were multiple bullet holes in the drywall and embedded in the bunched-up covers and mattress. Everywhere she looked there was destruction.

It was nothing short of a miracle that she and Joe hadn't been hit.

Or killed.

Her knees threatened to buckle. As if sensing her weakness, Joe slipped his arm around her waist, holding her upright. "Come on, Elly. Let's go."

She nodded. After taking a few steps, she grabbed her coat. When she lifted it up, she immediately saw there was a bullet hole in the garment. She dropped it as if it were a snake that would bite. "I—uh, this has been hit by a bullet. Can I wear it? Or do I leave it here?"

"Leave it." He looked upset, but then added, "We'll keep the squad warm for you. I'll have an officer stay inside with the motor running."

"Okay." She dropped the coat and continued to the open door. From the looks of the broken jam, she deduced Steele had kicked it in to gain access.

Rhy's tactical team to the rescue.

She managed to get down the stairs to the ground level where several cop cars were parked. The place was lit brighter than the Christmas parade. Joe led her to one and instructed the officer to keep the motor running. "Stay inside with Elly, understand?"

"Yes, sir."

Joe turned to her. "I'll need you to wait here, okay?"

She nodded, even though she didn't want him to leave her alone.

"This won't take long."

"I know." She slid into the back seat.

A flash of indecision crossed his features, but then Joe closed the door and turned away. She watched as Joe and Steele joined other officers milling around the parking lot. Then the two men disappeared from her line of sight.

She rested her forehead on the cool window, concentrating on taking slow, deep breaths.

The danger was over. If the shooter was smart, he'd have taken off. And if he wasn't smart, she knew Joe, Steele, and whoever else was out there would find him.

Yet she couldn't begin to comprehend why this was happening. Had the shooter targeted her simply because she'd bumped into him before the parade?

Because she'd drawn the sketch of his likeness that had been flashed all over every news channel, locally and nationally?

Or was it just because she was one that got away?

"You okay back there?" the cop behind the wheel asked.

"Yes." No, of course not. How could she be okay? How could anyone be okay after something like this?

Elly closed her eyes and sought peace in prayer, the way her parents and Rhy had taught her.

Please, Lord Jesus, keep us all safe in Your loving arms. Amen.

JOE HATED LEAVING Elly in the squad, but he had a job to do. The only way to keep Elly safe from harm was to find this guy ASAP.

"He had to have been up in a tree," Joe said to Steele as they crossed the parking lot toward the ridge of mature trees lining the opposite side of the parking lot from the building. "The angle of the bullet that hit the mattress indicated he was above the second-floor landing, shooting in a downward trajectory into the room."

Steele whistled under his breath. "The goal was to kill Elly."

"Yes. I have no doubt about that." It didn't make any sense, but this guy was clearly twisted, having absolutely no conscience as he ruthlessly killed innocent people. "I'm thankful Elly was in the bathroom."

"You think he used a scope?" Steele asked as they split up, walking about three feet apart into the wooded area.

"Must have." Joe scanned the ground searching for footprints. "Although if so, I would have thought he'd have noticed Elly wasn't there."

"Maybe he didn't look closely enough to realize the pile of blankets and pillows weren't a person." Steele shrugged. "He may have been too eager to take action."

"Maybe." Although he found that difficult to believe. This guy had proved himself to be a cold-blooded killer. Not a hyped-up kid dealing with a rush of adrenaline. "He's not the typical active shooter, that's for sure."

"Yeah, I'm getting that." Steele glanced at him. "Highly unusual for an active shooter to stalk a witness."

"Exactly. And how did he find her here?" Joe scowled. "I don't like it, Steele. Not one little bit."

"Agreed." Steele paused, then glanced upward. "This tree doesn't have a direct line of sight to the motel room. His position must have been closer to where you are."

Joe nodded. He forced himself to take a deep breath, then dropped to his haunches. He couldn't rush this. As much as he hated to admit it, their perp was smart. He'd taken extra precautions to avoid being caught. Which meant he would have taken care not to leave evidence behind.

Yet he'd also fired off several rounds. The chances were slim that he'd have been able to pick up all his brass. He'd heard Raelyn had found shells at the Christmas parade too. None with prints, unfortunately, but it was something.

He'd take whatever they could get.

A glint of brass caught his eye. A surge of satisfaction hit hard. "I have something. I need an evidence bag."

Steele crossed over to join him. "Here."

Using the bag as a glove, he picked up the shell casing. Then found another one. Only two, but that was a good start. Enough to match them as the same make and model Raelyn had found at the parade.

"Looks like he made another mistake," Steele said with a grim smile. "I believe he'll make more."

Joe didn't doubt that they'd find him. The question was when. It was already going on ten hours from the initial shooting event at the Christmas parade. They needed to find and arrest this guy, before he killed anyone else.

He was sick to his stomach knowing sweet Elly was in the center of this guy's crosshairs.

"Joe?" A male voice caught his attention. Rising to his feet, he turned to see Gary coming toward him, a look of alarm etched on his features. Joe inwardly winced, thinking about the damage that Gary's motel room had sustained.

"I'll pay for the repairs," he said quickly. "I'm sorry, Gary. I did not expect this guy to find us here."

"I have insurance." Gary waved an impatient hand. "That's not why I came out here. I feel somewhat responsible, for this mess too. I swear I was watching the cameras but never saw this guy."

He'd wondered about that. Turning, he stared across the parking lot. From this position, he could just barely make out the camera located on the second floor near the stairs that were positioned right outside Elly's room. At the time, he'd thought that room was the best for her. Close to the stairs leading down to the ground level and close to the camera that would alert them to danger.

Then he frowned. "Gary, has that camera outside the room been tampered with?"

"That's what I was trying to tell you." Gary looked upset, making Joe wonder if the guy was concerned about his relationship with Rhy. "I was watching the cameras and didn't see anyone. Not a single hint of movement. But I also didn't notice the one camera was pointing off at an odd angle."

"That camera right outside Elly's room." His heart sank.

"Yes, although I didn't make that connection." Gary's expression revealed his anguish. "I feel like I let you down, Joe. Rhy too."

"It's okay." Gary was a former firefighter, not a cop. He wouldn't think like a cop, no matter what the circumstances. That was his job. If anyone had failed here, it was him. Joe should have double checked that the camera was pointed in the correct direction.

"It's my fault," Gary muttered. "All my fault."

"It's not," Joe interjected. "The shooter did this, not you. And I should have noticed it too. I guess the good news is that he didn't target any of the other motel rooms."

Gary's jaw dropped as if that possibility hadn't occurred to him. The older man spun around to stare at the front of the motel. "You're right. It's only the room Elly was in that was destroyed."

"Yeah." And that, too, wasn't typical behavior for the typical active shooter. Joe would have expected the gunman to spray the entire front of the motel, taking out as many people and damaging as much of the structure as possible.

But he hadn't. No, the shooter had focused all his attention on Elly's room.

A shiver snaked down his spine as the implication sank deep. This guy was not playing around. Joe wasn't sure how they'd escaped this far. He would have to get Elly way off-grid to keep her safe.

He heard Steele on the phone and realized he was already checking with Raelyn, comparing the brass they'd found here to the ones she'd discovered at the scene of the Christmas parade.

"Yeah, okay. Thanks." Steele lowered his phone. "It's a match, at least make and model. We'll need forensics to compare in more detail."

"That's something. Although we can't connect the brass to the shooter unless we find the gun." Joe sighed. "Let's keep searching for evidence."

"Hey, I found something over here!" A uniformed officer waved his hand to get their attention. Joe and Steele jogged over.

"What is it?" As soon as the question left his mouth, he saw the barest hint of a footprint. It wasn't much, and he glanced up at the officer with a frown. "You sure this isn't from one of the dozens of cops roaming around?"

"I'm sure. We spread out in a grid formation." The young officer's gaze was earnest. "I think the shooter left it."

"Maybe." Joe wasn't completely convinced. "Go ahead and mark it. Keep your eyes peeled. Maybe we'll find another to match it."

"Will do." The young cop appeared anxious to please.

As he rose to his feet, Joe realized the news of Kyle Malaki's death must have spread across the cop community. Not that nailing a cold-blooded shooter wasn't motivation enough, but a cop killer always ratcheted up every officer's desire to apprehend a perp.

Whatever it takes, he thought with a grim sigh. They needed every cop in the entire city to be on high alert.

He began to walk toward the squad where he'd stashed Elly, but then he realized what he was doing. Checking on her wasn't necessary. There was still work to be done, and she was safe inside the squad.

Turning away, he caught Steele's arched brow and inwardly winced. Yeah, his fellow officer had noticed what he'd almost done.

Steele knew he was getting too emotionally involved.

Steele gestured him over. "You found the brass here, right?"

"Yeah." Joe swept his gaze up the tree. "I see what you're thinking. Give me a leg up."

Steele obliged by lacing his fingers together to make a stirrup. Joe stepped up into Steele's hands, then braced his hands on the tree trunk as Steele hoisted him up.

He caught the lowest branch, then pulled himself up to

climb the tree. As a kid, he'd loved climbing trees, but as an adult, he found it difficult to wedge himself between the branches. They were bare of leaves but still close together.

Sitting on the lowest branch, he eyed the motel. Nope, this wasn't high enough. He carefully stood and climbed higher. The next V was better, but as he eyed the distance, the angle of the shots that had pummeled the mattress still wasn't right.

"Anything?" Steele called.

"Not yet. Do you have a pair of binocs down there?"

"Yeah." Steele was dressed in his full gear, and he removed a small pair of binocs from his utility belt. "Ready?"

Joe leaned forward and caught the binocs with one hand. Then he moved horizontally from one branch to the other. Still not high enough. He sat for a moment, frowning. Was he wrong about the angle? It had all happened very quickly, and his concern had been on reaching Elly while avoiding being shot.

Then he glanced over to the other tree. The one to his left. Looking down at the ground, he thought it was more likely that the gunman had been up here. But he could be wrong. Still, he didn't give up on the tree until he'd crawled to several more possible positions.

"Are you taking a nap up there?" Steele asked.

"No." He gazed down at him. "This isn't the right angle. And I haven't seen any evidence that anyone else has been up here either."

"You said he had to be shooting from an elevated position," Steele said. "Which means he was up in a tree."

"I know. Look out, I'm coming down." After stuffing the binocs in his pocket, he carefully climbed to the lowest branch, then straddled it like a horse, turning upside down so he could drop to the ground. He scowled at Steele's grin. As a tactical unit, they often fought side by side in dicey situations. But there was also plenty of razzing between the guys—and gals, he silently amended—during downtime.

"I need another leg up." He gestured to the tree to their left. "I want to check this one."

"That branch is higher," Steele pointed out.

"Are you saying you're not strong enough to get me up there?" Joe challenged.

Steele scoffed. "Don't make me show you just how high I can toss your sorry behind." His buddy laced his fingers together again. "Come on, cowboy. Time to get in the saddle. Giddyap."

Shaking his head, Joe placed his boot in Steele's palms, then steadied himself as his buddy used all his strength to lift him up. He managed to grasp the branch and hung dangling for a moment before he was able to pull himself the rest of the way up. Climbing the tree was why he and the others hit the gym on a regular basis. All those pull-ups and push-ups had prepared him for this.

He swung his legs over the branch and sat upright. He sat for a moment, then pulled out the binocs and zeroed in on the motel.

A chill ran down his spine. This was it. This was the nest the shooter had used in his goal to kill Elly. It was the right height and distance.

He peered through the binocs, trying to envision the room past the bullet ridden glass. It wasn't easy, but he could make out the white sheets of the bed.

Twisting on the branch, he looked down and could see the area where he'd found the brass.

Scanning the surrounding area, he tried to imagine the path the shooter had taken to escape. He turned so that he was facing the large trunk of the tree and saw some scrape marks in the bark.

Oh yeah, this was it.

There was a smooth part of the tree trunk that he'd have checked for prints. Even though the guy at the parade had been wearing gloves, it was worth a try. Gazing past the tree trunk, he saw the church. "Steele? Did anyone go through the church?"

"I'll check." Steele lifted his hand to his radio to make the call. "Attention all units, who cleared the church?"

"I did," someone responded. "Five minutes ago. It was clear."

Five minutes. Too long, Joe thought with a frustrated sigh. It had taken them too long, and now the shooter was once again in the wind.

CHAPTER FIVE

Elly's fingers hurt from being laced so tightly together to keep them from trembling. She felt safe in the squad, but watching as uniformed officers combed the area and rolled crime scene tape across the stairs leading up to her bullet-ravaged motel room only made her aware of how close she'd come to dying here tonight.

Joe too.

Turning in the seat, she tried to look through the rear window to see where Joe was. There was no sign of him, though, just the officer named Steele who had come to their rescue standing beside a tree.

Joe abruptly dropped to the ground next to him. Startled, she realized he'd been up in the tree. Was that where the shooter had been? Shivering, she thought that likely.

She needed to call Rhy, but her phone was up in the motel room. She leaned forward to catch the officer behind the wheel's attention.

"Um, excuse me? Can one of the officers bring my phone down? I left it up in the room."

The officer grimaced and shrugged. "It's a crime scene.

You won't be able to get your phone back until it's been cleared."

"And how long will that take?"

He shook his head. "At least a few hours, maybe more. They're taking photos now, but then will want to find every slug they can."

"Okay, thanks." She sat back and reminded herself that the phone was easily replaced. For all she knew, it had been broken by flying bullets or drywall debris. It was just the waiting that was getting on her nerves. Doing nothing while others searched for the evil man who'd done this.

She startled badly when a dark shape loomed outside the window. Then recognizing Joe, she relaxed and tried to smile as he opened the door. He dropped into a crouch near the door. "Hey. Are you okay?"

"Sure." Her voice sounded shaky, and she hoped he didn't notice. "Did you find anything?"

He nodded and reached inside to take her hand. The warmth of his fingers helped calm her nerves. Everything about him exuded confidence, and she knew without a doubt that Joe and the other members of the tactical team would do their job. "We're finding evidence, which is good. But no sign of the shooter yet."

"I figured." She felt certain the atmosphere around the crime scene would have changed dramatically if the shooter had been found and taken into custody. "I saw you drop out of a tree."

"Yeah." His gaze held hers. "That's where he was when he opened fire on your room."

The statement made her shiver, and his fingers tightened around hers. "I—guess it's good you found that."

"Every little bit helps." His smile was sweet. "Oh, that reminds me." He released her hand to pull out his phone.

After swiping at the screen, he handed it to her. "Your brother."

"Joe? What's going on?" her brother asked.

"It's Elly. I—we're at the American Lodge, but the gunman showed up. He—we're okay, Rhy. No one was hurt. But Gary's motel room is in shambles."

"How were you found?" Rhy asked, his voice tense with fear and worry. "I'm glad you're okay, Elly, but I need to talk to Joe."

"Okay, here he is." She handed the phone back to Joe.

"There's no sign of the guy," Joe said into the phone. He listened for a moment, and she could imagine Rhy grilling him for information. Sure enough, Joe gave him a quick summary of the shooting event.

She missed Joe's warm touch but reminded herself that he was working. His job was to find this guy and arrest him. Not to waste time comforting her.

"Yeah, Rhy, I get it. Trust me, I thought we were off-grid, but obviously not." Joe's tone was laced with frustration.

"Tell him we're fine," Elly said. "None of this is your fault."

Joe didn't do as she'd asked. After a long pause, Joe said, "I plan to leave my SUV here and to ask Steele to give us a ride. But we'll need a replacement vehicle by morning." Another pause, then, "Yes, that works. I'll be in touch. Do you want to talk to Elly again?"

Her brother must have said yes because Joe handed her the phone. "I told you we're fine. No one was hurt. And this isn't Joe's fault."

"I never said it was," Rhy drawled. "But I'm trusting him to keep you safe, El. This shooter shouldn't have found you once, much less twice."

Difficult to argue that. "What about Devon and Colleen? I know Steele was keeping watch at the homestead; he was the first one to get here. I need to be assured your family is safe too."

"We're fine. Raelyn is here, keeping watch," Rhy assured her. "Besides, I think it's pretty clear this guy is after you, Elly. Not us."

"Why? That part doesn't make sense."

"I don't know." Rhy sounded just as frustrated as Joe. "This guy doesn't have the same MO as most active shooters."

And that wasn't good. Rhy didn't say the words, but they reverberated through her head anyway.

"Elly? Are you sure you're okay?" Her eldest brother's voice pulled her from her troubled thoughts.

"Yes. Joe is doing everything possible. We'll be in touch when we can. Just so you know, I don't have my phone. It's part of the crime scene."

"You and Joe need to get different phones anyway," Rhy said. "But that will have to wait until tomorrow too. Be careful. Get some rest."

"You too. Bye." She ended the call and handed the phone back to Joe. "Thanks."

He nodded and glanced over as Steele approached.

"Area has been cleared, you and Elly can leave anytime," Steele said. "You mentioned wanting a ride?"

"Yes." Joe straightened. "My SUV is parked alongside the building, but I can't take the chance the shooter noted the plate number, so I'm leaving it here."

"Understood." Steele glanced around, then added, "Stay here. I'll run back to Rhy's place and get my vehicle."

"Thanks," Joe said.

She slid out of the back seat of the squad to stand beside

him. It was all she could do not to throw herself into his arms. She turned, her gaze going back to the tree. What had gone through the shooter's mind when he sat up there, aiming at the motel room window?

Maybe nothing. His cold, dead eyes made her think he didn't have any emotions. No good ones anyway.

She shivered and folded her arms across her chest. To her surprise, it didn't take long for Steele to pull up, well beyond the perimeter that the cops had set up around the motel. Joe's phone dinged, and he glanced at the screen.

"That's Steele. Let's go." He curved his arm around her waist, urging her forward. She caught a few curious gazes aimed at them as they crossed the parking lot.

Five minutes later, she was settled in the back seat of Steele's SUV. "Do you have a destination in mind?" Steele asked.

"Yeah. The City Central Hotel." Joe glanced back at her. "Have you been there?"

"No." But her siblings had. "I've heard it's nice."

"They have two-bedroom suites," Joe said. "And it's far from Brookland."

"You want me to book it under my name?" Steele asked.

"That would be good." Joe agreed.

Steele took a moment to call to reserve the suite. Thankfully, they were accommodating despite the late, or rather, early hour. They'd been at the hotel for several hours, but this close to the winter solstice, dawn hadn't brightened the day yet. Sunrise was a good three hours away.

Joe sighed. "I still can't figure out how he found us at the American Lodge."

"You're sure you weren't followed?" Steele asked as he drove through the suburban neighborhood.

"I did everything possible to shake a tail." Joe looked thoughtful. "Although if he was using a scope, who knows?"

"We cleared the scene, so heading to the City Central Hotel should work," Steele said.

Steele headed straight for the interstate, which was blessedly empty at this hour. Elly felt herself relaxing against the seat cushions.

The trip down to City Central took about fifteen minutes. She glanced around curiously as Steele pulled in. It was a step up from the American Lodge, but not by a lot. She knew from her siblings that the DA's office used the place for their witnesses, keeping them close for trial.

Joe got out of the car, then opened her door. He took her hand as they followed Steele inside. She told herself not to overreact to the simple, kind gesture.

Steele obtained the keys, then escorted them to the room. She belatedly realized Steele had a computer case with him, setting it on the small table. The suite was nice, with bedrooms located on either side of the small living space.

"I need to get back." Steele clapped Joe on the shoulder. "Keep your head down."

"You too." Joe walked Steele to the door, then closed and locked it behind him. He turned to face her. "Are you hungry?"

"Not really." She headed toward the closest bedroom. "We should try to rest."

"Sounds good." He held her gaze for a long moment. "Good night."

"Good night." She entered the bedroom, closing the door behind her. The darkness outside should have helped her fall asleep.

It didn't.

Elly tossed and turned, then gave up. It was no use. Slipping out of bed, she pulled the blanket off and eased into the main living area. The sofa faced a TV. She turned it on, instantly decreasing the volume so as not to wake Joe.

He needed to sleep more than she did.

She curled up in a corner of the sofa and tried to focus on the movie playing on screen. It was, of course, a Christmas movie, one she normally loved.

The sound of a door opening startled her. She turned in time to see Joe emerge from his room. "Can't sleep?"

"No." She gestured to the television. "I hope I didn't wake you."

"You didn't." To her surprise, he crossed over and dropped beside her. "I was worried you'd have nightmares."

"That's the reason I was in the bathroom when the shooter opened fire." She sighed. "And likely why I can't fall asleep, now."

"Elly." He said her name on a sigh and wrapped his arms around her shoulders. "I wish you weren't stuck in the middle of this mess."

She leaned gratefully against him. "I'm glad you're here with me."

"Always." He drew her closer still.

She buried her face in the hollow of his shoulder. She knew Joe was just being kind and supportive because Rhy was his boss, but breathing in his musky scent made her wish for something more.

Much more.

LISTENING to Elly's deep breathing, Joe smiled when he realized she'd fallen asleep. Holding her like this was incredibly wonderful and pure torture at the same time. No matter how much he wanted to kiss her, she was Rhy's baby sister and, therefore, off-limits.

He'd promised his boss to treat her with the respect and professionalism she deserved. And he would.

Even if it killed him.

His thoughts went back to the shooter. The sketch of his likeness had been all over the news. What was the point of silencing her now? Sheer revenge? Seemed like a huge risk considering the guy had escaped the scene of the Christmas parade without being caught.

He needed to dig deeper into the victims, specifically Gabrielle and Henry, the ice skaters. The more he thought about this perp, the more he believed the guy had either military or cop training. Maybe Gabrielle had a former boyfriend or husband who fit the profile.

Steele had left a laptop for him to do some digging, but he didn't want to disturb Elly.

Yeah, he was in trouble. Deep trouble. But that wasn't enough to make him move away. No, instead, he rested his cheek against Elly's hair and closed his eyes.

He must have slept because he awoke when she shifted against him. He blinked, noticing the sun had finally risen enough to lighten the room. Elly stirred in his arms but then seemed to relax again. He was glad she was getting some rest.

He eased away from Elly, gently setting her prone on the sofa. She was beautiful, even in sleep. He tore his gaze from her with an effort.

Enough. There was work to do. He knew from Rhy all about the Finnegan family reunion and Christmas party Elly had planned—he glanced at his watch—one week from today.

They needed to find this son of a gun and toss him behind bars well before then.

He took a moment to clean up in the bathroom, then tiptoed to the small table. Seeing the coffee maker, he glanced back at Elly, wondering if making a pot would wake her up.

Forcing himself to wait, he opened the laptop and powered it up. The noise made him wince, but Elly didn't stir.

Taking that as a good sign, he opened a browser and began to dig into Gabrielle and Henry's social media pages. Unlike him and a lot of other cops, the skaters had a huge social media presence. He supposed that went along with being professional athletes.

Ignoring the rumbling in his stomach, he began reading the comments. Someone, likely a public relations rep, had posted the news of the devastating death of Gabrielle and the critical injuries suffered by her partner, Henry.

Every comment, and there were literally hundreds of them, were messages of shock, sympathy, and grief. After going through half of them, he decided to switch gears.

The shooter wasn't going to post on social media that they deserved what had happened to them. He was smarter than that.

If their perp knew Gabrielle on a personal level, it was more likely he'd be featured in previous posts. Not the most recent ones. He scrolled through them, overwhelmed by the sheer number, and tried to find any photos of Gabrielle with a man who wasn't Henry, her ice-skating partner.

After a solid twenty minutes, he had nothing to show for his efforts. Then he realized he should be looking at their personal pages, not their professional ones.

Mentally kicking himself for being stupid, he found

Gabrielle's personal page. To his surprise, that one wasn't private. And he found one photo with Gabrielle smiling into the camera with a man beside her. He stared at the image for a long moment, but the guy's face didn't match the sketch Elly had done.

Still, he made a point of digging further to find the guy's name. Keith Daniels. He made a note of the name, then checked the simple case search to see if the guy had been in trouble with the law. Since he didn't have a date of birth, the results were inconclusive.

He'd have to check with Steele on whether he could find any intel on the guy. He didn't honestly think Gabrielle's boyfriend, if that's who Keith was, would have hired the shooter to do the deed. But they needed to cover all their bases and follow up on every possibility.

No matter how remote.

"Joe?"

Hearing Elly's husky voice sent a ripple of awareness shimmering down his spine. He glanced over to find her sitting upright on the sofa, her auburn hair mussed from sleep.

"Hey." He smiled. "You look better after your nap."

"It was nice to sleep without dreams," she admitted.

Her comment hit him hard. He hated knowing she'd suffered nightmares after the shooting event at the parade. Granted, her nightmare had meant she wasn't lying in bed when the guy had taken his third attempt to kill her. "I'm sorry about the nightmares, Elly. They'll get better over time, but you may need to see a specialist."

"I've considered that." Her smile was sad. "It seems wrong to be so traumatized when others lost their lives. Their loved ones."

"Everyone suffers in an event like this." He longed to

pull her into his arms for a kiss but stayed where he was. "Don't downplay the actions you took last night. You ran into danger to help others."

"Surprised myself," she murmured. "Basically, I acted without thinking." She hesitated, then added, "Honestly, a lot of that was because of you being there too. When I saw Kyle lying on the ground, bleeding, I feared the worst."

He tried to think of something else to say. Her comment about his being there was humbling. They'd both done their jobs, yet here they were, spending time together because the danger was still out there.

"I know God was watching over us, Joe."

He nodded slowly. He knew the Finnegan family was big into their faith and church. He used to attend church as a kid, but that had changed when his father began drinking. Maybe he needed to reconsider going back at some point.

She yawned, covering her mouth. "No coffee?" She looked disappointed.

"I held off because I didn't want to wake you." He jumped up, anxious for something to do. "I'll make it now."

"Thanks." She rose and tugged the blanket off the sofa. "I'll be back in a few."

He nodded, busying himself with the in-room coffee service. What was wrong with him? He needed to bring his emotions down a notch. Or two.

Or ten.

He'd known Elly for years. Granted, he'd only gotten to know her a little better during this past year when it seemed the Finnegan family was constantly in danger. He needed to think of her as Rhy's baby sister.

When Elly emerged from the bathroom, he knew his attempt to keep her at arm's length was failing badly. Yet he did his best not to let his feelings show. He poured a cup of coffee for her, then found the powdered creamer and sugar that he knew she liked. "Here you go."

"Thanks." She smiled gratefully as she doctored her cup and took a sip. Then her gaze darted to the computer. "What are you doing?"

He drank his coffee black, the way most cops did. He set his cup near the computer and dropped back into his seat. "I'm digging into Gabrielle and Henry's social media posts. I keep thinking there might be a reason she was the first victim."

"Can I help?" Elly pulled the other chair over to sit beside him. He wanted to protest, but of course, he couldn't.

"Sure." He took another sip of coffee, then tapped the screen. "I found a photo of Gabrielle and this guy, Keith Daniels, from a year ago."

"They look close," Elly admitted. "But he's not the shooter."

"I know." He was glad Elly sounded so certain. She was the only witness they had so far that had been close to the shooter. "I'll keep going back in time, maybe we'll find another picture featuring our perp."

"It never ceases to amaze me how many people put their entire lives online for anyone to see," Elly murmured, a frown puckering her brow. "Rhy always made it clear we needed to stay off social media to protect the family."

"I can understand that." Most cops didn't want their information out there either. And Rhy was always protective of the younger siblings. "Safer that way."

"I know." She smiled. "I wasn't quite so understanding as a teenager, though. I remember wishing I could be on the same sites as my friends."

He didn't know Elly as a teenager; he hadn't transferred to the tactical team until four years ago. She'd just turned twenty, he remembered, and even then, he'd thought her cute.

Five years, he reminded himself. He was five years older than she was. She needed to date someone like that guy Derek. The one she'd claimed was too young.

The guy he'd instantly hated on sight when he'd thought they were seeing each other.

He forced himself to focus on finding a clue about the shooter. Not on Elly as a possible date.

"It's a good policy to keep your personal life private," he said. He pointed to the screen. "And this is why. Look how easy it is to find information on Gabrielle, without leaving the hotel room."

"You really think Gabrielle knew the shooter?" Elly asked. "He didn't strike me as the kind of guy who made a habit of watching figure skating."

"It's one theory." *Among others*, but he kept that to himself. "And he wouldn't have to be the kind of guy to watch it to have dated Gabrielle."

"I guess." She leaned in to see better, making him wish there was a second computer. She was far too close for his peace of mind.

Doing his best to remain professional, he continued scrolling through Gabrielle's posts.

"Hold on a minute." Elly covered his hand with hers. "Did you see that?"

"What?"

"There was something about another pair of skaters." She pushed his hand away from the mouse pad to maneuver the pointer. "Here. This post here is about how Gabrielle and Henry beat out Alicia and Thomas White for the number one slot."

"Yeah, but there's always someone who is going to come

in second place, right?" He didn't see this as a big deal. "Everyone can't win."

"I know but read through the comments." Her voice held a note of excitement. "It sounds like this is a long-standing rivalry."

He could see what she meant, but he still wasn't impressed. "Okay, maybe these two couples were rivals on the rink, but this Thomas White guy doesn't look like our shooter. And I think it's a stretch to believe Thomas and Alicia would hire someone to shoot Gabrielle at the Christmas parade."

She turned to look at him. "Remember Nancy Kerrigan and Tonya Harding? Tonya convinced her ex-husband to take a police baton to break Nancy's leg."

He arched a brow. "How long ago was that?"

"Years." She waved a hand. "I only know about it because I like watching ice skating. The announcers have mentioned it a few times, even though I think that happened back in the early nineties."

Well before Elly was born. But he understood her point. "Okay, maybe you're right. It might be wise to consider the rivalry as a motive to the crime."

"A drastic solution," Elly agreed. "At least Tonya Harding only injured Nancy Kerrigan. She didn't have her murdered."

Murdered. Was it possible a professional rivalry could have caused this? He hated to admit it wasn't a stretch. These days people tended to solve their disagreements with violence rather than common sense and calm conversation.

It was a lead, one they desperately needed.

CHAPTER SIX

Elly sipped her coffee, trying not to let her gaze linger on Joe. Being held in his arms had been wonderful; his strength had comforted her. She almost wished she hadn't fallen asleep, but obviously she'd needed the rest. She'd never again take sleeping without nightmares for granted. She empathized with those who suffered PTSD from their role as a cop or in the military. Those were the people who put their lives on the line every day to protect the public—people like her.

Being here in the City Central Hotel suite with Joe made her feel safe.

Oddly, she found him more handsome in his casual clothes rather than his uniform. Maybe because she was accustomed to seeing him in uniform, as he was usually working when he was at the homestead. He was always nice to her from a professional perspective.

Without the uniform, he seemed more approachable. He hadn't shaved, and the stubble on his cheeks only added to his attractiveness. But even as the thoughts whirled in her mind, she knew better than to make a big deal out of being here with him.

Joe was here because he'd promised Rhy he'd keep her safe. His loyalty was to her brother, and she could respect that.

Even though she would rather have had more.

"I'll get this information about the rivalry to Steele." Joe's words interrupted her thoughts. "It can't hurt to interview the skaters' parents."

"Will you get to help with that?" He was close enough to touch, and she would have loved to lean against him. But she reminded herself that she was a Finnegan. Maybe she wasn't a cop like Rhy, Tarin, and Kyleigh or an FBI agent like Brady, but she wasn't a weakling either. She wanted to do her part in bringing this guy to justice.

He shrugged. "Maybe. We'll see." He abruptly stood and moved away, stretching his arms over his head. "In the meantime, are you hungry?"

"Yes." She glanced around the room. "Are we staying here or going out?"

"Staying here where it's safer." He frowned. "We'll order room service. Just tell me what you'd like."

Leaning forward, she plucked the room service menu from the desk. "The breakfast special sounds good." She handed it to him.

He scanned it, then nodded. "That works." He reached for the phone and placed their order.

"What else can we do to find this guy?" she asked when he'd finished. "I'm sure the police have more access to information than what we can find on social media."

"You'd be surprised," he said with a sigh. "We can uncover a lot if they have criminal backgrounds. If they don't, we only have what's out in the general public." He gestured to the computer. "Which is what we've been doing here."

"Wow." Somehow, she'd thought they'd have more. "Okay, then we keep digging. The rivalry is only one possibility, right? You initially thought the shooter might be Gabrielle's former boyfriend or spouse."

"That reminds me." He returned to sit beside her. "I meant to access the public records to see if Gabrielle had been married."

She watched as he brought up a new search window. After a few minutes, he shook his head. "Okay, no marriage or divorce on file. That means this guy may have been a former boyfriend."

"That won't be easy to nail down," she murmured.

"No." He glanced at her, and their gazes clung for a long moment before he looked away. "Here, you keep poking around on Gabrielle's social media sites. I—uh, need to call Rhy about obtaining a car."

Joe moved away to make the call. She continued scrolling through Gabrielle's posts but without much success. If the skater had a former boyfriend who matched the description of the shooter, he wasn't in any of the photos she could find.

Joe's conversation with her brother was brief, and she only heard his side of things. "A rental SUV under the Callahan name would be great, Rhy. Let Matt Callahan know we appreciate the help."

"Matt Callahan?" she asked. "He's the K-9 officer of the Callahan clan. He has a beautiful German shepherd named Duchess."

"Yes, I've met them, they're quite a team." He smiled. "Matt will rent the vehicle for us, but your brothers Colin and Quinn will drop it off."

"Sounds good." It seemed her entire family was pulling together in this, and she appreciated their support. "I didn't see Matt at the parade, was he there?"

"He was but was stationed toward the end of the parade route." Joe shook his head. "There wasn't much of a scent trail for Duchess to follow, but they assisted in searching for the perp anyway. Unfortunately coming up empty-handed like the rest of us."

It was disheartening how the shooter managed to get away. Then again, disappearing in the midst of chaos wasn't that difficult. All he would have had to do was to run and act frightened, blending in with everyone else who fled the scene.

A knock at the door had Joe rushing forward, waving her back. Without protest, she stood and moved toward the bedroom as he squinted through the peephole.

"Room service," a muffled voice said.

She watched as Joe opened the door just wide enough to take the tray. He set it on the table, passed some cash over, and then closed and locked the door.

Elly willed her pulse to return to normal. She wasn't used to this. She didn't normally look for danger around every corner the way Joe did. The way her cop siblings did.

"Time to eat," he said calmly, as if he hadn't acted like a shooter had arrived at their door.

She moved forward as he shut the computer and removed it from the table. He removed their dome-covered meals from the tray. She moved her chair over to give him room.

"I would like to say grace," she said when he dropped down beside her.

He nodded and bowed his head.

She reached over to take his hand. "Dear Lord Jesus, we

thank You for this food we are about to eat. We humbly ask that You continue to keep us safe in Your loving arms. Amen."

"Amen," Joe murmured.

She reluctantly released his hand, glancing at him as she uncovered her plate. "I wasn't sure if you would want to pray."

"I haven't been to church in a long time," he admitted. "But I know the Finnegans are big believers."

She nodded. "We are. And I believe it's only because of God's grace that we're safe now."

"Maybe." He didn't say anything more as he dug into his food. She wanted to press the issue, but that really wasn't her nature. Either Joe would believe or he wouldn't. She couldn't force him.

"When do you think we'll hear from Steele about when he may be able to interview the skaters' parents?" She steered the conversation back to the investigation.

"Hopefully soon." He glanced at his watch. "If he doesn't reach out by the time we're finished eating, I'll call him. To be fair, I only just sent him the information an hour ago."

"Right." She grimaced. "Seems like days ago, doesn't it?"

"Yeah." He sipped his coffee. "We also need to wait for your brothers to arrive with the rental."

"Will members of your tactical team continue to watch the homestead?"

"Absolutely. Raelyn handed that task over to Grayson earlier this morning." He offered a faint smile. "Don't worry, everyone is bound and determined to protect Rhy's family."

"That's good to hear." She needed to believe her family

would be safe. Well, as safe as possible under these circumstances. "I worry most about Colleen."

"We all do." His tone was sincere. "Try not to stress, okay?"

"Okay." She finished her scrambled eggs and bacon. Based on the danger they'd lived through in the past twelve hours or so, there was no way to know when they'd have a chance to eat their next meal.

Despite feeling safe here with Joe, she honestly didn't expect the peace and quiet to last for long. Better to anticipate the shooter's next move.

If that was even possible.

The sound of Joe's phone ringing startled her. She carefully set down her coffee cup. Cutting down on the caffeine might be a good idea.

"Hey, Colin." Joe listened for a moment, then nodded. "Fifteen minutes sounds good." He gave her brother their suite number, then disconnected from the call. "They're bringing replacement phones too. Along with a winter coat for you and extra cash."

"Finnegans to the rescue," she said lightly. She knew from stories at Sunday dinner that her siblings had this sort of thing down to a science by now.

She took a moment to wash up in the bathroom while waiting. When Colin and Quinn arrived, they both engulfed her in a big hug.

"Glad you're safe, kiddo," Quinn said.

"Yeah, what he said," Colin joked, but his gaze was serious. "I can't believe you were in the middle of that mess."

"I'm glad I was able to help."

"Elly was amazing," Joe said. "She saved my life, rescued a small boy, and offered first aid to many other victims."

"That's our sis," Quinn said. Then his smile faded. "I can't believe you saw the shooter, up close and personal, El."

"Your sketch was great," Colin added.

She wasn't used to so much praise from her siblings. They'd always supported her, but up until now, she hadn't done anything impressive. Other than graduating from her EMT program. "You brought phones?"

"Yep." Colin set them on the table. Then he tossed the car key fob to Joe who caught it easily. "The SUV is black and parked closest to the exit."

"Thanks. We appreciate the support," Joe said.

Her brothers stood for a moment, and she imagined some silent he-man eyeballing going on between them, before they turned to leave.

"Call if you need anything else," Quinn said as they opened the door.

"We will," she assured him. "Thanks again."

She wanted to tell Joe not to pay attention to her brothers, but he was looking down at his phone. "Steele is on his way. He wants to talk."

"Okay." She was grateful to have the tactical team's support, along with that of her siblings. "I'll get the phones ready."

"Thanks." Joe placed the laptop on the desk, then went back to work while she activated the new phones. Fifteen minutes later, Joe's phone buzzed. He glanced at the screen in satisfaction. "Good. He's here."

Steele was still wearing his uniform. And while he was handsome, too, with his dark hair and blue eyes, she didn't feel the slightest flicker of attraction. Why, she asked herself silently, did she want the only man who wasn't interested in her?

"Elly." Steele acknowledged her with a nod.

"I hope you haven't been working all night." She frowned. "You need to get some sleep."

"I slept for a few hours," Steele assured her. Then he turned to Joe. "I spoke with Michaels about the interviews you suggested. I was able to convince Gabrielle's and Henry's parents to come down to the station in about an hour."

"I'd like to participate in the interview," Joe said. Then he glanced at her, and added, "Since the interviews are taking place at the precinct, I could bring Elly with us. She'll be safe there."

Steele arched his brow. "Michaels agreed to have you there, but I'm not sure how he'll feel about bringing a civilian along."

"I'm not some civilian, I'm the one who saw this guy, remember?" Elly stood straighter, leveling Steele with a hard look. "I'm invested in this as much as you are."

"She's right," Joe said. "Besides, you know I can't leave her here. I'm sure Michaels will get over it."

"Fine." Steele threw up his hands. "I'll drive you both in my vehicle, okay?"

"Thank you." She donned the winter coat Quinn had brought her. Maybe she didn't know much about police work, but she was involved in this mess up to her eyeballs.

And she had a bad feeling this nightmare wouldn't end anytime soon.

TAKING Elly along with them to the police precinct probably wasn't smart. He could have asked Colin and Quinn to come back and stay with her at the hotel.

But truthfully, he couldn't bear to let her out of his sight.

Joe knew Steele was concerned about his ability to remain objective. And maybe his colleague had a right to be worried. When their food service had arrived, he'd almost pulled his gun on the guy.

Not cool. He needed to find a way to ignore this constant awareness he experienced with Elly and stay focused on the investigation.

"How is the tip line coming along?" Joe asked.

Steele grimaced. "Lots of calls that haven't yet provided anything helpful. There was one guy who claimed he saw the perp getting into a pickup truck, and since we know that much already, we figure he did see our shooter. He gave us two letters off the license plate, but the list of possible matches is long since the only color option we have is a dark vehicle. We don't dare narrow it down to a specific region."

"I get that, but it's a start." He perked up at that information. "I wouldn't mind poking around on the list. Maybe we'll be able to match a registration to a driver's license photo."

"Working on that," Steele agreed. "Can't hurt to have another pair of eyes on the list."

They reached the precinct without any trouble. By tacit agreement, he and Steele kept Elly between them as they headed inside.

"Hey, Delaney, Gabrielle's parents are in interview one," an officer called out.

"Great," Steele said. He looked at Joe, then added, "Let's get Elly in a cubicle."

"I'd rather listen to the interview," she protested.

"Afraid not," Joe said. "I'll let you know if we learn anything interesting."

She didn't look happy, but he couldn't let that prevent him from doing his job.

He took a moment to change into his uniform, to make it official that he was on duty. Then he and Steele entered the interview room.

"Mr. and Mrs. St. John, I'm Officer Joe Kingsley, and this is Officer Steele Delaney. We are very sorry for your loss."

"It's been awful." Gabrielle's mother had clearly been crying. "We'll do anything to help you find our Gabby's killer."

"Thanks, we appreciate that." He and Steele sat across from the couple. "We need to know if your daughter had any enemies? Or maybe a jealous boyfriend?"

The parents exchanged a look. "There was one guy, Bart Shaw," her father said. "He went off the deep end when Gabby broke up with him."

"Can you be more specific?" Joe leaned forward. "We need to make sure he's not involved in this."

"Oh, he doesn't look like that sketch on the news," Gabby's mother said with a sniffle. "I'm sure about that."

"Bart called Gabby for weeks, showed up at rehearsals, and generally made a nuisance of himself," her father said. "But after I confronted him and let him know Gabby was going to get a restraining order, he backed off."

"Bart short for Bartholomew?" Steele asked. "Not a very common name."

"I think he was named after his grandfather," her mother said. "But I'm telling you, he doesn't look anything like that sketch."

"Okay, we appreciate the information. What about anyone else bothering your daughter?" Joe pressed. "I saw something about a rivalry between Gabrielle and Henry and another pair of skaters."

"Oh, that's nothing." Gabby's father waved a hand. "A publicity stunt dreamed up by their PR teams."

Joe glanced at Steele, who shrugged. He turned back to Gabby's parents. "Are you sure about that? With Gabrielle and Henry out of the competition, Alicia and Thomas White are likely to be ranked in first place."

Gabby's father frowned. "Anything is possible, but Gabrielle and Henry didn't think the rivalry was anything serious. I can't imagine Alicia and Thomas White hiring someone to kill our daughter."

"But what if they did?" Gabby's mother's eyes filled with tears. "Oh, Rob, do you think it's possible?"

"I don't know." Gabby's father put his arm around his wife's shoulders.

"I was the one who pushed Gabby to skate," her mother said between sobs. "If I hadn't, she'd still be alive . . ."

"You can't think like that," Gabby's father said. He looked at Joe with tired, grieving eyes. "If the rivalry between the skaters was a big deal, Gabby didn't let on. She downplayed it, much the way she did her breakup with Bart. She was so sweet and innocent . . ." It was his turn to break down, closing his eyes and pressing his face into Gabby's mother's hair.

Their overwhelming grief was tangible. He glanced at Steele who didn't seem to have any more questions for them either.

"Thank you for your time," Joe said. "Again, we're very sorry for your loss."

The older couple managed to pull themselves together long enough to leave the interview room.

Joe shook his head. "That was rough."

"Yeah," Steele agreed. "I doubt the interview with Henry's parents will be much easier."

"We need to check out Bartholomew Shaw," Joe said. "He should be relatively easy to find."

"On it," Steele said in agreement. It didn't take long for the guy's picture to show up on the screen. "Yeah, he's definitely not our shooter." His buddy turned the phone so that he could see the man's image.

The man on the screen had a round face, a small chin, and a stocky frame. "He could have hired someone."

"Maybe," Steele agreed. "We'll bring him in for questioning too."

Joe got the impression they could be there all day. Which wasn't a bad thing, as the sooner they could weed some of these suspects out, the better.

The interview with Henry's parents was even less enlightening. They were just as broken up as Gabby's parents, yet clinging to hope that he might survive despite being in the ICU and listed as being in critical condition.

Bart Shaw was easy to find as well. He claimed he had nothing to do with Gabrielle's murder or the shooting at the Christmas parade. Steele hammered him pretty hard, going over and over his alibi for the time frame in question, but the guy stuck to his guns.

Having nothing concrete, they were forced to let him go. Yet as soon as they were alone, Joe said, "We need a subpoena to dig into his financials. No way is he the shooter Elly bumped into and that I glimpsed running from the scene. But he could have hired someone."

"Possibly," Steele agreed. "Hard to imagine him doing that, though. Honestly, he seemed rather harmless."

"We need to make sure." Joe wasn't about to take any shortcuts here. Not with a case of this magnitude. "Check with Michaels to make sure he's on board. Hopefully, the judge won't balk at a subpoena."

"He won't," Steele said confidently.

They rose and left the interview room. He noticed Elly was sitting exactly where he'd left her, chatting with a rookie cop. He had to squash the flash of jealousy. He turned to Steele. "Do you need my help with the subpoena?"

"I'll take care of it." Steele nodded toward Elly. "Looks like she needs to be rescued from Alan. Give me a few minutes to get the ball rolling, then I'll drive you both back to the hotel."

"Thanks." He headed toward Elly, noticing with a surge of satisfaction that he had no business feeling how her eyes lit up when she saw him. Without hesitation, she murmured something to the rookie, then stood and edged past him to meet him halfway.

"You've been gone a long time." She searched his gaze. "I hope you learned something helpful."

"We did." He tried not to smile at how crestfallen the rookie looked at how quickly Elly left him. He cupped his hand beneath her elbow. "According to both Gabrielle's and Henry's parents, the rivalry thing was more of a PR stunt than anything serious."

"Really?" She looked disappointed. "I had hoped it would lead to a possible suspect."

"Oh, we'll still dig a little deeper into Alicia and Thomas White, just to be certain," he assured her.

"You didn't learn anything else?" She looked disappointed.

"We interviewed one possible suspect, but that's about it." He nodded to where Steele worked away at a computer. "He's working on a subpoena. We're heading back to the hotel as soon as he's finished."

"Okay. That would be great."

He felt guilty for making her sit there for so long. The hour was well past noon. He should have asked her brothers to stay with her rather than dragging her down to the station with them. He wondered why no one had issued a shelter in place order. Although that would be difficult to do for a city this size. Still, Elly should be sheltering in place as much as possible.

Next time, he silently promised himself.

"Kingsley?" Steele glanced over with a grin. "We got it. We should have access to the information in a couple of hours."

"Great." He gestured to the closet chair. "Sit tight for a minute while I change."

"I'll stand. I've been sitting enough."

"Understood." He hurried to the locker room to change. He would have preferred to stay here working, but it was Sunday, and he was already racking up overtime. Maybe tomorrow he'd convince Elly's brothers to take over guard duty for a while.

Ten minutes later, he was ready. Steele glanced at him as he approached. "Are we heading out the front or the back?"

"The back," he said. "Maybe you can drive your SUV around to meet us?"

"Sure thing." Steele didn't argue.

"I don't suppose we can grab something for lunch on the way," Elly said as she shrugged into her winter coat. "It sounds crazy, but I'm hungry."

"We can, but you'll have to settle for fast food," he warned.

She wrinkled her nose but nodded. "Okay, that's fine."

He gave Steele two minutes to drive around back, then headed that way with Elly. He opened the door a few inches to make sure Steele was there. When he saw him, he opened the door wider. "Let's go."

She eased past him, taking only one step when the sharp crack of gunfire rang out.

"Elly!" He grabbed the back of her coat and dragged her back into the relative safety of the building, wondering how the shooter had known where to find them.

CHAPTER SEVEN

She'd felt the bullet whiz past her ear, embedding itself in the doorframe just inches away from her head. The close call robbed her of speech. Joe had hauled her back inside the precinct, quickly slamming the door shut as if anticipating more shots.

But she didn't hear anything.

Sliding to the floor, she wrapped her arms around herself to keep from falling apart. She still had trouble understanding why anyone wanted her dead. She'd been told she was a people person, great at interacting with others.

But this wasn't personal. The shooter didn't hate her personally. His goal must be to eliminate her as a witness.

As if listening through a long tunnel, she heard the muffled sounds of Joe yelling for officers to search for the shooter. No way. She wasn't going to pass out. There wasn't any blood!

With sheer determination, she lifted her head to look up at him.

"Elly! Are you hit?" Joe dropped beside her, raking his gaze over her.

"I don't think so." She struggled to push the words past her tight throat. "I felt the bullet whiz past, though. I—think it's in the doorframe."

His gaze darkened, and he nodded. "We'll get it out, see if we can match it to the slugs pulled out of the American Lodge motel room. Steele and others are out searching for him right now."

"Okay." She struggled to draw in a deep breath, willing her heart rate to return to normal. "How did he know we were here?"

"I don't know." Frustration laced Joe's tone. "This shouldn't have happened."

That seemed to be the common theme with this guy. She lowered her head to her knees, praying for strength. She was alive and so was Joe. This guy had not succeeded in killing again.

Yet.

"Hey. It's okay." Joe's voice radiated concern as he crouched beside her. "We're going to find him."

"I know." She drew in another breath and lifted her head to face him. "It's just that a police precinct should be a safe place."

"Yes, it should be." Joe hesitated, then said, "He took a chance shooting at you here. It's his first big mistake. I'm confident we'll find him."

She nodded, taking heart in that thought. "Yes, that's how most criminals are found, by their mistakes."

"Exactly." Joe's blue gaze held hers. "We'll match the slug in the door here to the others. We'll slowly but surely build a case against him. And once we have him in custody, he'll never see the light of day again."

He sounded so confident she couldn't argue.

"Can you stand? I'll help you."

"Of course." She injected confidence into her tone. She wasn't a weakling. And she wasn't hurt. Joe stood and held out his hand to help her up. The warmth of his fingers wrapping around hers helped steady her nerves. She rose to her feet with a little boost from him. "Thanks."

"Oh, Elly." He abruptly pulled her in for a tight hug. She clung to him, but just that quickly he released her. "Let's go. I'll find some body armor for you."

"Wait, what?" She frowned. "That's not necessary." She didn't add the part where body armor wouldn't have prevented that bullet from going through the center of her forehead. Feeling the tremors return, she opened and closed her hands, willing the feeling to go away.

"It is." Joe didn't so much as glance at her. He clearly wasn't in the mood to listen to reason. "We're taking every precaution possible."

They already had been doing that with marginal success. She decided there was no point in putting up a fuss.

"We need the smallest one they have," Joe muttered as he sent through the few spare vests in the equipment room. "It won't be specifically fitted for you, but that would take time we don't have."

His phone rang, and he quickly pulled it out. "Steele? Do you have him?"

The crestfallen expression in Joe's eyes indicated the news wasn't good. She moved forward to search through the vests herself.

"No sign of his brass either?" Joe threaded his fingers through his hair. "How many possible locations could he have used to take that shot?"

Another long silence as he listened to Steele's explanation. She held one vest that seemed smaller than the others to her chest. It was still too big, but it would have to do.

"Okay, thanks for trying. Have the others keep scouring the area, but I need you to get us out of here." Joe eyed the vest she held, nodded and continued talking. "We need a different vehicle. Grab one of the undercover cars, anything that has four-wheel drive will work."

She examined the straps of the vest, trying to figure out how to slip it on.

"Thanks, Steele." Joe ended his call, slipped his phone into his pocket, then reached for the vest. Within thirty seconds, he had secured it around her torso. "It's not perfect," he muttered under his breath. "But it's better than nothing."

She tugged at the vest, surprised by how heavy it was. It gave her a new appreciation for how Rhy, Joe, and the other officers ran after bad guys while wearing this along with the rest of their gear. When Joe moved toward the door, she grabbed his arm. "Wait. You need a vest too."

"I know, mine is in my locker." He tipped his head toward the door. "I'll grab it, and then we'll meet up with Steele to get out of here."

Of course, he had a vest, one specifically fitted for his muscular build. Obviously, she wasn't thinking clearly. Blame it on being shot at. "Sounds good."

She lingered outside the locker room while Joe grabbed his vest. Then they met up with Steele, who looked seriously ticked off.

"I checked the obvious locations, the trees directly across from the precinct's back door," he said in a grim tone. "But there are also several houses in that area, and this guy could have been up on one of the rooftops. I knocked on every door, but no one claimed to have seen anything. Without a warrant, I couldn't search them."

"Useless to get a warrant now," Joe said. "This guy is long gone. I doubt he's left evidence behind inside the house."

"That's what I thought too." Steele sighed. "I can't believe he had the nerve to try this here."

"A mistake," Joe corrected. "He's an arrogant son of a gun, I'll say that much. But still a mistake. He'll make enough of them that will lead us straight to him."

"I hope you're right about that," Steele groused. "Because it feels like he's taunting every cop who works in the city."

Joe's expression turned thoughtful. "That may be another clue, Steele. If he's a former cop or former military, then he may have a grudge against his former colleagues."

"That doesn't explain why he shot Gabrielle, Henry, and so many other innocent victims," she felt compelled to point out. "They're not in law enforcement."

"Yeah, there's that," Joe admitted. "He hit Kyle, but most of his victims were not cops."

The images of the bleeding and dying victims flashed in her mind. Gabrielle. Henry. The elderly man, the young man cradling his wife to his chest . . . so many.

Too many.

"Boss gave me the keys to an undercover SUV," Steele said, breaking into her heartbreaking memories. "Do you want to head out back again?"

She was about to protest, but to her surprise, Joe nodded.

"Yeah, that works." Joe nudged her forward. "You and the rest of the guys have made sure he's not back there. That makes it the safest exit at the moment."

"Okay, I'll head out first. Give me two minutes." Steele led the way back to the rear door.

She followed Joe. "Where are we going?"

"The hotel." He glanced at her over his shoulder. "We've been safe there, Elly. I have to believe this guy has law enforcement background. Maybe he recognized me and knows this is my district. He likely staked the place out, hoping we'd return."

"That makes sense." Another thought occurred to her. "Or maybe he followed Gabrielle's parents here."

Joe's eyes widened with admiration. "That's brilliant, Elly. I'm sure you're right about that. I bet he anticipated we'd come together to interview them."

Her cheeks grew warm at his praise. She silently prayed he wouldn't notice. Seriously, she needed to get a grip. He'd been oblivious to her secret crush for months now, and she needed it to stay that way.

"One more minute." Joe glanced at his watch. "I'm going to step out first. You're going to stay directly behind me, okay?"

She wanted to protest but knew it would be useless. She stood behind him, waiting for him to open the door.

The seconds ticked by slowly. He abruptly opened the door and moved across the threshold. She couldn't see much beyond the breadth of his shoulders. "Stay close," he repeated as he took another step.

She gripped the back of his leather jacket and followed him away from the safety of the building. They only took five steps before reaching the SUV. Joe opened the back seat for her, so she quickly climbed in.

Soon they were back on the highway. She frowned when she noticed they were heading in the wrong direction.

The City Central Hotel was near the courthouse, which was east of the precinct. Not west.

"Where are we going?" she asked.

"You mentioned food," Joe reminded her. "We're going to circle around the city to get something before returning to the hotel."

"Oh yeah." She wasn't hungry anymore but held her tongue. Nothing like being used for target practice to ruin a girl's appetite.

Yet to her surprise, when they picked up their meal, the scent of french fries made her mouth water. Okay, maybe she was getting better at bouncing back after facing adversity.

The roundabout trip to the hotel didn't take as long as she anticipated. Steele dropped them off near a side entrance, and Joe protected her with his body as they entered the building, leaving Steele to drive around to the front to park.

In the suite, she ditched her coat and began pulling off the vest.

"Don't," Joe said sharply. "You need to keep that on."

"Even in here?" She glanced around the suite.

"Yes, always." His tone was firm. "I'm not taking another chance with your life."

"Joe." She reached out to touch his arm. "You're doing everything possible, and I appreciate that. But you must know I'm not afraid to die. I mean, I don't want to, but if that's God's plan, then so be it. I know I'll be home with the Lord."

He stared at her in horror. "Don't talk like that," he choked.

She dropped her hand and turned away. She had been telling the truth.

Yet it bothered her that Joe didn't share her faith in God's plan.

———

SHE WASN'T *afraid to die.* The words echoed through Joe's mind, sending a chill down his spine. This wasn't right. Elly shouldn't be in this situation. None of this was her fault.

Yet all the wishes in the world wouldn't change the facts. Elly was in danger. This shooter had targeted her.

No way was he letting this guy get that close to hurting her again.

"Have faith, Joe," she said quietly.

He wanted to have faith that God was watching over them. That they'd find this guy before he hurt anyone else. But Joe believed more in hard work than divine intervention.

But he nodded, then headed to the door to let Steele in.

"We should eat before it gets cold," Steele said, dropping the bag of food on the table. "Besides, I'm hungry."

"That's fine." He pulled another chair over to the small table as Steele pulled their sandwiches and fries from the bag.

"I'd like to say grace," Elly said, taking the seat next to him.

He glanced at Steele, expecting him to balk, but his fellow cop simply shrugged.

Elly took his hand, then bowed her head. "Lord Jesus, we are grateful for Your presence in keeping us safe from harm. We thank You for blessing us with this food and with Your guidance as we seek justice. Amen."

"Amen," Joe echoed. Maybe she was right about having

God's protection. He couldn't explain how this guy who'd killed so many had missed Elly on three separate occasions.

"Amen," Steele said. Then he popped a fry in his mouth. "I think we need to review our notes on this case. There must be something we're missing."

Joe couldn't agree more. "Elly made a good point about the shooter possibly following either Gabrielle's parents, Henry's parents, or even Bart Shaw."

Steele arched a brow. "That makes sense. Although he still made the assumption that we'd bring Elly to the precinct for those interviews."

"Yeah." He took a bite of his burger, trying to think of any other way this guy could have found them. "Do you think he has a two-way radio? Maybe listening in on the cop frequency?"

"Could be, but I'm confident no one mentioned Elly over the radio." Steele shrugged. "I'm thinking our perp dug into the Finnegan family. Plenty of stories on the news about them over the past year."

"That's true." Joe had been involved in a few of the situations but not all of them. Although he would have been there if asked. He and the rest of the tactical team would do anything to support Rhy. He was by far the best and most honorable boss they'd ever had.

Which made these attempts against Elly all the more difficult to comprehend.

"Maybe it's time to call my brother, Brady," Elly said.

"He's with the FBI, right?" Steele asked. "Not sure Michaels will go for that. The feds tend to be stingy with information."

"Normally, I'd agree with you. But Brady is a Finnegan," Joe said. "He'll be more interested in helping to protect his sister than taking over our investigation."

Steele grudgingly nodded. "Okay, fine. We can use all the help we can get."

"And then some," Joe muttered half under his breath. The fact that they hadn't gotten a hit on facial recognition with Elly's sketch bothered him. If this guy was former military or law enforcement, they should have his name, rank, and serial number by now.

"Let me call Brady," Elly suggested, rising to her feet. He noticed she only ate half her sandwich and fries.

She moved into her room to make the call. Joe watched her go, then felt Steele kick him under the table.

"Be careful, Kingsley," Steele warned. "You're letting her mess with your head."

"I'm fine," he shot back. "She's Rhy's baby sister, and I promised to keep her safe."

"That's my point. You're getting emotionally involved, which is a surefire way to fail in that mission."

Since he knew Steele was right, he swallowed another protest. "I know," he admitted quietly. "I'm doing my best."

"Try harder," Steele suggested bluntly. "Seriously, buddy, you cannot let your emotions cloud your judgment."

"I won't." He hoped that if he silently repeated that to himself often enough, it would come true. Steele wasn't telling him anything he didn't know. He quickly changed the subject. "Do you have any other ideas for finding this guy?"

Steele stared at him for a long moment as if trying to see into his brain. Thankfully, he let the issue of Joe's not-so-subtle feelings for Elly go. "We can follow up on the forensic evidence, but that isn't going to help until we find the weapon to compare. At this point, our only option is to continue focusing on the victims."

"We need Shaw's financial records." It seemed unlikely

the guy had hired their shooter to kill Gabrielle, but stranger things had happened.

"Yeah, but not likely on a Sunday," Steele said.

"Maybe Brady can pull some strings on that too," he said.

Elly returned to the table. "Brady agreed to work with his tech expert, a guy named Ian, to see if he can use AI technology to create a three-dimensional human version of my sketch to send through their facial recognition program."

"That would be great." He was glad she'd made the call. "Any idea on how long that will take?"

She grimaced. "Not sure. He planned to reach out to Ian right away, but it is Sunday. And Ian was working on a missing child case from prior to the parade shooting. We may not hear back until tomorrow."

He tried not to chafe at the delay. This wasn't a TV show where things just magically happened in record time. Yet this guy had killed at least ten people in a mass shooting.

But a missing child was also a priority. Hard to justify letting go of that case to work this one.

Steele stood and began gathering garbage together.

"Elly, finish up." Joe pushed her half-eaten meal toward her. "It's better to eat now since we never know what might happen later."

"Okay." She sat, then tugged on the vest, clearly uncomfortable wearing it. She seemed to attack the remnants of her meal, eating it without really tasting it.

He couldn't help but admire her grit and determination. She might look all soft and sweet and feminine, but she was also stronger than the rest of the Finnegan family gave her credit for.

Something she'd proven over and over again in the past eighteen hours.

Steele's warning flashed in his mind, so he stood and grabbed the laptop computer. He dropped onto the couch and booted the device up.

Work. He needed to stay focused on the case. It was good that they had a few leads to follow, but there also wasn't time to kick back and relax.

The key to this disaster had to be within the victims. This guy had taken out the skaters first for a reason.

If this was a random attack, it didn't make sense that he would continue to stalk and shoot at Elly.

As he opened one of the popular social media sites, he frowned. "Steele, who is pouring through all the street camera footage?"

"I'm not sure who Michaels assigned that to," his colleague admitted. "Why? Is that something you want to do?"

"It occurs to me that Elly might be able to pick this guy out on camera better than anyone else." He glanced at Elly who nodded.

"I'd be happy to do that."

"Okay. I'll see what I can do." Steele pulled out his phone. "Should I have the video sent to a specific email?"

"Use mine," Joe said. "I'll pull it up on the laptop for her."

Steele made the call. Joe was glad to have another angle to investigate. He hadn't been kidding about the shooter making mistakes. He'd already left slugs and brass behind. They had a decent sketch, and every cop in the city and surrounding areas were on the lookout for him.

It was only a matter of time before they had their perp in custody.

"Okay, the video is on the way," Steele said.

"Great." Joe pulled up his email program and logged in.

Elly sat beside him, seemingly anxious to help. He ignored all the messages, including one from his former girlfriend, Tina, and waited impatiently for the video to drop.

"Who's Tina Landry?" she asked.

"An old friend." He wasn't getting into his previous relationship with her now. Tina had left him for a rich guy who'd slapped her around. Now she wanted Joe back. It had been over eight months ago, and all he felt for Tina was sympathy for her suffering an abusive relationship. Whatever feelings he'd once had for her were long gone. "Here's the video."

The video quality wasn't great. The city of Milwaukee had several budget shortfalls in the past few years, which meant many cameras were broken or had been damaged in some way. Many of those cameras that were working had grainy screens.

"That's the video?" Doubt laced Elly's tone. "I'll do my best."

"I know you will." He smiled and set the computer on her lap. "That's all we can ask."

She went to work, taking her time and viewing the video in slow motion so she wouldn't miss anything. He forced himself to leave her to it, standing up and moving away from the sofa.

"That was a good idea on the video, Kingsley." Steele cocked a brow. "Every little bit helps."

"Tell me about it," he muttered. "I'd like you to pull some strings getting Bartholomew Shaw's financial records." He rubbed his stubbly jaw. "It would be nice to take him off the list if he's not involved."

"I'll try." Steele still held his phone in his hand. "But I still think the feds have more juice to get that done."

"I'd rather they focus on the sketch," Joe said. "Having

an ID on this guy would be huge. Frankly, that's the quickest way for us to find him."

"Yeah, okay." Just as Steele was about to make the call, his phone rang. Steele put the call on speaker. "Yeah, boss?"

"A pickup truck was found four blocks from the precinct," Michaels said. "I want you to head out there ASAP."

"What makes you think it was left by our shooter?" Joe asked. He knew there were witnesses at the Christmas parade who thought the guy had escaped in a dark pickup truck. But there were hundreds of them in the area.

"A witness said a guy matching the sketch got out of the vehicle, taking off on foot." Michaels sighed. "The truck was left in an area where the citizens are not usually anxious to help the police. But I think the parade shooting was bad enough for the caller to report it. He refused to give his name or address, though. Just the general location of the vehicle."

"I'm on my way," Steele promised, already making his way to the door.

"Good. Keep me posted," Michaels added.

Joe made sure to lock the hotel room door after Steele left. When he turned around, he frowned when he saw Elly had left the computer on the sofa and was gone.

Despite Steele's warnings blinking like red neon signs in the back of his brain, he crossed over to make sure she was okay. When he heard her sniffling, he winced.

Had the video of the Christmas parade caused another flashback?

"Elly?" He rapped on the door to her suite. "Are you okay?"

She didn't answer. Alarmed, he tried the handle. It wasn't locked.

"Elly. I'm coming in." He pushed the door open and saw her sitting on the edge of the bed, a tissue pressed against her eyes. "Hey, don't. I'm sorry. I shouldn't have made you watch the video."

"I volunteered." Her voice was muffled behind the tissue. She took another from the box beside her, blew her nose, and stood. "I'm okay now. For some stupid reason I was caught off guard, but I can do this."

"You don't have to . . ."

"Yes, I do." She took one last swipe at her face and stood. "This is important. I'm not just afraid for my family but for all the other potential innocent victims still at risk."

She came toward him, looking beautiful despite her red nose and puffy eyes. Then she slipped her arms around his waist and hugged him.

Her embrace touched a chord deep within. He pulled her close, wishing she wasn't wearing the bulky vest. "I'll help you review the video," he whispered.

She pressed her face into his neck, and a wave of desire washed over him. He tried to loosen his arms, but she lifted her head, went up on her tiptoes, and kissed him.

The minute her lips touched his, Steele's warnings evaporated into mist. They were well into the danger zone now. Yet that didn't stop him from angling his head to deepen their kiss, wanting her in a way he hadn't thought possible.

CHAPTER EIGHT

Joe's kiss was far better than she'd ever imagined it would be. As his arms tightened around her, and he deepened their kiss, she reveled in the fact that he wasn't treating her like Rhy's baby sister now.

No, he was kissing her like a woman he wanted.

The buzzing of his phone was like an annoying wasp. Joe abruptly broke off their kiss, breathing heavily as he fumbled for the device.

"Rhy," he said in a hoarse voice.

Of course, her brother would ruin this moment, interrupting their first—but hopefully not last—kiss. Finnegans didn't curse, but she wanted to when Joe dropped his arms and stepped back to answer the call. He put at least three feet between them as if fearing her brother might be able to see how close they were standing.

"What's up?" Joe asked, avoiding her gaze. His reddened cheeks made her want to smile.

"Put the call on speaker," she said, moving closer.

"Ah, Elly wants to hear this too." Joe looked adorably

knocked off kilter as he continued backing out of the room, heading to the sofa.

"What's this about gunfire at the precinct?" Rhy demanded. "What in the world is going on, Kingsley?"

"Steele and I were interviewing the parents of the ice skaters because we learned of a rivalry between those who were shot and another pair of skaters," Joe explained. "I was taking Elly outside through the back after we'd finished when the shot rang out. She's fine, no one was hurt."

"Did you find him?" Rhy sounded extremely frustrated.

"Not yet." Joe kept his gaze on the phone as if unable or unwilling to meet her gaze. "Steele and several other cops ran out to search the area but didn't come up with anything. Steele paid extra attention to the trees across the street since we know he used a tree to shoot at the American Lodge but didn't find anything. There is a row of houses that are directly across the street from the back side of the police station. They canvassed the area, but you know how that neighborhood is, Captain. The residents rarely cooperate with the police. No one admitted to seeing anything."

"I can't believe this guy had the gall to stake out a police station," Rhy muttered harshly. "That took some nerve."

"I know, but I'm fine," Elly said. "Steele left to check out an abandoned truck a few blocks from the scene."

"Oh yeah?" Her brother's tone didn't sound encouraging. "That may not mean much in that neighborhood either."

"One witness came forward, saying a guy matching the description of Elly's sketch got out of the truck," Joe explained. "The vehicle will be processed ASAP. We can only hope the guy left some trace evidence behind."

"I think we'll all pray for that," Rhy agreed. "I don't like the way this guy keeps coming after Elly."

"I'm wearing a bullet-resistant vest that Joe gave me from the precinct," she said, before Joe could respond. "I promise he's doing a good job of keeping me safe, Rhy."

"I know, I know." She could understand Rhy's frustration. "I just don't get this guy's motives. I mean, shooting up the parade to get attention is one thing. Continuing to stalk and kill a witness is highly unusual."

"We're going to find him," Joe said. "He's made a few mistakes already; he'll continue to make more. And we have Brady working with his tech guru on some AI software that will take Elly's sketch and create a three-dimensional image to put through the bureau's facial recognition program. We'll find him," Joe repeated. "Count on it."

"I'm counting on you keeping Elly safe and on the rest of the team finding this perp," Rhy said with a sigh. "I'm glad you've gotten Brady involved. We need all hands on deck for this."

"I couldn't agree more," Joe said.

"I spoke with Eloise, Kyle's wife. She's pretty broken up over his death. She's in the anger phase of her grief, yelling at me to do something to find her husband's killer."

She winced. "I'm sorry you had to go through that."

"Part of the job," Rhy said. "I didn't take her anger personally. All I could do was reassure her we were doing everything possible to find the perp."

"Do you think some of the team members should stop out to check on her?" Joe asked.

"I offered that," Rhy said. "But she told me she didn't want to see anyone from the tactical team until the guy was either dead or in custody."

There was a long silence as they digested that bit of information. Joe still hadn't met her gaze, which irked her.

They were two adults who'd shared a kiss. There was nothing wrong with that.

"Need anything else?" Joe asked.

"No." Now Rhy sounded tired. In the background, they could hear Colleen crying.

"Take care of your family, Rhy," Elly said. "Don't worry about us."

"I will. Keep me in the loop," Rhy added, before ending the call.

Joe abruptly shot off the sofa, putting even more distance between them. She frowned, not liking his abrupt about-face. "I—uh, should apologize."

"For me, kissing you?" She arched a brow. "Not necessary. I enjoyed every moment."

Her blunt statement caught him off guard. Then he turned and scooped the laptop off the sofa. "Let me check the video. If I see someone who looks like our perp, I'll let you know."

She sighed as he returned to the table with the computer. Clearly, he regretted their kiss. Which was depressing since she didn't.

This probably wasn't the best time to talk about it, especially having just finished speaking to Rhy. Yet she cherished their all-too-brief embrace.

Maybe one day, when this nightmare was over, she could talk to Joe about the possibility of seeing him again. Not related to work.

"Elly?" She glanced over when he called her name. "Check this out."

She didn't need to be asked twice. She hurried over and pulled up a chair to sit beside him. He clicked play to unfreeze the section of video he had up on the screen.

The video wasn't great, but she caught a brief glimpse

of the shooter's face seconds before he merged into the crowd. "That's him," she said with certainty. "Can you pick him up in another part of the video?"

"Let's see." Joe shut down that video and picked up the next one. She realized each video was from a different camera.

It wasn't easy to sit there, watching how people ran every which way. There was no sound, but she could tell by the open mouths of several parade attendees that they were screaming.

"This isn't the right angle," she said. "He's already gone by now."

"Okay, I'll try another." Joe clicked on the next video. This was from a camera mounted at a busy intersection. When a dark pickup truck drove through the intersection, Joe hit the stop button. "Do you think this could be him?"

She waited as he backed up the video and ran it again, slower. The truck rolled slowly past, but while she could see there was a dark shadow of a driver behind the wheel, it was impossible to identify him as the shooter.

"I don't know," she admitted. "What about the license plate?"

"Let's see." Joe manipulated the video again and was able to capture the license plate. "Looks like this matches the truck found near the precinct."

She nodded. "Call it in to Steele."

Joe did so but was forced to leave a message. She sat back in her seat, doing her best not to let the images of the chaos on the screen get to her.

"I hope Kyle's wife never has to see this," she said in a low voice. Then she turned toward Joe. "When I saw him lying in the street, bleeding, I had a horrible moment when I thought he was you."

Joe's blue eyes darkened. He was close enough to kiss, but she managed to refrain. They still had work to do. "I'm sorry you had to go through that."

"We all went through it." She forced a smile, remembering her overwhelming relief at discovering Joe wasn't injured.

Then she frowned. What had Kyle said when he looked up at her? He'd called her name, Elly. Then he tried to say something more but only managed to say the beginning of her name, El. She'd thought he was still referring to her, but now she couldn't help but wonder if Kyle had been trying to say his wife's name. Eloise.

Sadly, she wished he had been able to give his wife a message. Maybe one last declaration of love. It might have helped ease her pain and anger just a bit.

Unfortunately, whatever Kyle had wanted to say died with him.

"WAIT, did you say Kyle said your name?" Joe asked. This was the first he'd heard of Kyle saying anything after being shot.

"Yes. He recognized me." Elly's expression was one of grief. "I felt so bad for him, Joe. I tried to reassure him that I'd take care of him, but he was bleeding so much. There wasn't anything I could do."

"Try to remember the lives you saved, Elly, rather than those you couldn't." Easy to say, he knew, but not as easy to believe. "This perp shot ten people in cold blood. There's nothing either of us could have done to prevent that."

"I know." She shook her head and sighed. "I just feel bad for his wife, that's all."

Joe forced himself to tear his gaze from hers. Having her sitting this close where he could still breathe in her enticing scent made it extremely difficult to resist the temptation to kiss her again. Especially after the way she'd basically told him she had no regrets over their embrace. He had not anticipated the way her kiss had rocked him back on his heels.

Okay, if he were honest, he didn't regret their kiss either. Well, except for the thought of Rhy finding out about it. Just the idea of his boss walking in on them was enough to cool his desire.

Elly was an adult, almost twenty-five years old. But Joe knew full well that making a pass at Rhy's little sister was a sure way to get fired.

And pummeled by Rhy's fists.

Steele was right about not getting emotionally involved. Cool professionalism was the best way to keep Elly safe.

Unfortunately, it was too late. He already was emotionally involved, despite his best efforts to keep her at arm's length.

His phone rang, startling him. Glancing down at the screen, he saw Steele's name. Clearing his throat, he answered. "What did you find in the truck?"

"It's been wiped clean, which is suspicious. There is a little mud in the back of the truck bed, though, so the lab is going to test the sample to see if there's a way to match it to the area near the parade."

Noticing how Elly leaned closer to hear, he lowered the phone and placed the call on speaker. "Matching the soil sample seems a stretch," he said. "But what about the license plate? Elly and I found a shot of the truck's license plate. I left that information for you in a voice mail."

"Yeah, I heard the message, but it's not a match to this

truck. Did you get a good look at the driver? Did he look like our guy?"

"No, I couldn't identify him," Elly said. "So you're saying the truck we found was likely someone else, not the shooter."

"I don't know, we're running the plate number you gave us. Hang on a minute," Steele said. Joe heard muffled sounds of talking in the background, then he came back on the line. "Okay, we got a hit. The license plate you gave us was for a black Chevy truck that was reported stolen."

Joe couldn't say he was surprised. This guy had clearly planned to go on this shooting rampage, and stealing a truck would make it that much harder to track him down.

"The abandoned truck was also stolen," Steele continued. "It belongs to an older gentleman by the name of Fred Kettle. Grayson is there now. Hang on, he's texting me." There was another pause before Steele continued. "Okay, the guy's truck is in his driveway, and the license matches the plate number you gave us."

Swapping license plates was a criminal trick as old as time. "That proves the truck found near the precinct was used by the shooter." Joe smiled with satisfaction. "He changed license plates to slow us down."

"That's affirmative," Steele agreed. "I'm not sure why he left the vehicle behind, unless he figured it was easier to disappear on foot. Unfortunately, he didn't leave behind any other evidence as far as we can tell. We'll have the crime scene techs go over it in more detail, but I'm not expecting much. I'm sure he was wearing gloves. Maybe even a hat to limit the possibility of leaving hair behind."

"Yeah, okay." Finding the abandoned truck wasn't as helpful as he'd hoped, but having even this small piece of the puzzle helped. The big picture would emerge sooner or later. "We know he stole a truck, changed license plates, and then abandoned it. Can we check the street cameras to see if this guy got into another car?"

"That's being done, so far there's only a grainy image of a guy wearing a ski mask running away from the abandoned truck," Steele said. "No way to get facial recognition from the image."

"I wonder why he didn't wear the ski mask at the parade?" Elly said with a frown.

"He may have had one but didn't want to use it right away." Joe shrugged. "He likely believed he blended into the crowd better without it."

"Maybe," Steele said. "But he wasn't banking on Elly's keen instincts in recognizing a bad guy when she saw one."

The admiration in Steele's tone grated on his nerves. Which was probably why Steele had made the comment in the first place. Just another way of reminding Joe to keep his head screwed on straight.

"I bumped into him," Elly said modestly. "Only because I was admiring the Christmas lights. I was polite, but he looked angry."

"And that was another mistake," Joe said. "He should have smiled and moved on, but instead, he didn't bother to hide the evil in his heart."

"Did you find anything else on the video?" Steele asked.

"Nothing helpful," Joe said.

"We're still waiting to hear from Brady," Elly added. "I know they're busy with a missing kid, but I'm sure they'll get my sketch created into something that can be used by their facial recognition system soon."

"Yeah, okay. We're still checking a few things here," Steele said. "I'll let you know if we find anything more."

"Thanks. We'll talk more later." Joe disconnected from

the call. It bothered him to be sitting here with Elly rather than out on the street working the case.

All because Rhy had asked him to take care of his baby sister. And what had he done with that trust? Crossed the line by kissing her as if there was no tomorrow.

"I was hoping for more." Elly sighed. "It seems like progress is going slower than normal."

Joe had the same frustration. Especially in a case this big. "There's a lot being done, but this guy was smart enough to cover his trail."

"I know." She turned back toward the computer. "Should we keep going?"

"Sure." He swallowed hard and brought up the next video.

It was slow, painstaking work, but it had to be done.

"I need a break," Elly said. She abruptly stood and moved into the living area, dragging her fingers through her hair.

He felt guilty all over again for putting her through this. "I'll keep searching for evidence," he said. "You should relax for a bit. Try to take your mind off this."

"Impossible," she said on a sigh.

As much as he wanted to go over and offer comfort, he forced himself to stay put, not moving an inch. Comforting Elly was what had gotten him into trouble earlier.

He knew better than to make the same mistake twice in a matter of hours.

Yet he was hyperaware of how she paced the room, tugging on the uncomfortable borrowed bullet-resistant vest. There was a lot of video footage to get through, so he did his best to stay focused.

But after another hour, his vision blurred, fatigue catching up with him. He stood and stretched, blinking to clear his vision. He belatedly realized darkness had fallen outside. No wonder his eyes were burning.

He switched on a light, surprised to find Elly curled in the corner of the sofa, staring out at nothing. When the light came on, she pushed the blanket aside and stood.

"Hey, you're not wearing your vest." He crossed over to pick it up from the other end of the couch.

"Do you expect me to sleep in it?" She sounded cranky. Then she came toward him to take it from him. "Fine, I'll put it back on. But I'm not wearing it to bed."

"That's fine." He had already checked out her room, there was nothing across the street from her bedroom window that could be used as a nest for the shooter. And that was if he even knew about this place, which Joe was pretty sure he didn't. When he saw her struggling to get the vest on, he stepped forward. "Let me help."

"I don't know how you guys wear this every day," she groused. "It's hot, heavy, and extremely uncomfortable."

"You get used to it." For him, it was part of his uniform. For Elly, it wasn't. When he'd secured her vest, he took a step back. "Are you hungry? We can order dinner."

"I guess." She sighed, then added, "Yes, we should eat. I think we need to be ready if there's a break in the case."

After what happened down at the precinct, he wasn't taking her along with him anytime soon. But there was no point in starting an argument. He wasn't all that hungry either, but it would give them something to do. "Why don't you check the menu? I'm sure you can find something good."

She crossed to the desk and examined the limited room service menu. "I'll have the grilled chicken sandwich."

"Okay, I'll have the same."

The room seemed smaller somehow. The glow of the

lamp made it more intimate. He kept his distance, walking off the stiffness from sitting so long.

When Elly had finished placing the order, she turned to face him. "Food will arrive in thirty to forty minutes."

He nodded. "I should keep working, then."

"I really thought we'd hear from Brady by now," she murmured. "I had high hopes for the facial recognition idea."

"He'll get to it." Joe shared her impatience, but the fact that the shooter was on the loose but hadn't taken out any other innocent targets—other than attempting to shoot Elly—had caused the news anchors to move on to the next crisis.

The last time he'd checked the news feed on his computer, the media was still interviewing victims of the parade shooting and putting out notices about the missing kid that Brady was searching for.

He couldn't help but wonder if their perp was watching the crying victims being interviewed on camera.

What was this guy's motive? The way this had unfolded still nagged at him.

Returning to the computer, he picked up where he left off with the camera video. There were only three more videos to review. Which was good and bad.

They desperately needed a lead.

"I'm not sure what you think you're going to find," Elly said, coming over to sit beside him. "Look at those cars. With the glare from the Christmas lights, it's impossible to make out people's faces."

He shrugged. "Won't know that for sure until I check them all."

She fell silent but continued to watch the videos with him.

A knock at the door startled them both. He rose and

checked the peephole before opening the door. He took the tray, dug some cash from his pocket, and handed it over. "Thanks."

"You're welcome." The server pocketed the tip and quickly left.

Their meals arrived in a timely manner, making him wonder if the hotel wasn't very busy. Which was odd since it was a week before Christmas.

A Sunday, though, so weekend visitors had likely already checked out.

"I'd like to say grace," Elly said. Since he was used to her doing so, he nodded and allowed her to take his hand. "Dear Lord, we are humbled by Your gift of this food. And we ask that You continue to keep those searching for this evil man safe in Your care. Amen."

"Amen," Joe echoed. But he found himself silently adding another prayer of his own.

Lord, keep Elly safe too.

He hadn't prayed in a long time but oddly felt better afterward. As they dug into their respective sandwiches, he silently acknowledged that he cared about Elly.

Far more than as a friend. Or Rhy's younger sister.

"You know," Elly said, breaking into his thoughts. "I was thinking about that mud Steele mentioned on the back of the truck."

He glanced at her. "Don't get your hopes up, Elly. The chances of matching it to anything in the area of downtown Milwaukee are slim to none."

"No, not that." She looked thoughtful. "When I saw the shooter standing behind you and shouted at you to get down, he looked larger than life."

He nodded, remembering those seconds all too well. "Yes, I thought he looked as if he were standing up on something. But the truck?" He saw the connection she was making. "How could he have gotten the truck so close to the parade route?"

"I wish we could go back and walk the area again," Elly said. "I'm sure he was standing inside the truck bed. That's why he had such a clear view of the parade."

He reached across his sandwich to bring up the map application on the computer. He typed in the closest intersection to the parade route, then zoomed in on the screen. Elly leaned close too.

"There!" Her voice lit up with excitement. "See that strip mall? I wonder if he had the truck parked there earlier."

He had to admit she had a point. "You're thinking he left the truck there, then came back to use it as a pedestal from which to shoot."

"Yes. Because I was standing near here." She pointed to another spot on the map. "This is close to the location where I bumped into him." Her gaze met his. "And when he turned to leave, he walked away from the parade. Not toward it, but away."

To the truck. Joe could easily see that in his mind. But even knowing where the guy was standing didn't help much.

They were still no closer to finding him.

CHAPTER NINE

Elly stared at the frozen video screen, wishing she'd paid more attention to where the guy had gone after they'd bumped into each other in those moments before the parade has started. It had been a chance encounter, but she'd experienced a flash of apprehension.

Even then, she'd known he was evil. And he'd proved it by opening fire and heedlessly killing and injuring innocent bystanders.

Rhy was always saying they should trust their gut instincts. Mostly in relation to police work. Yet obviously, she should have heeded his advice that fateful night.

"I wish I'd said something back then," Elly murmured.

"That wouldn't have changed anything." Joe reached out to take her hand. "I told you that, remember? Telling me some guy concerned you wasn't enough. Not when you didn't see a gun or any sort of weapon."

"I didn't see anything resembling a gun. Especially not the semiautomatic weapon he lifted and aimed at you." She lifted her gaze to his. "He must have had the weapon hidden within his long coat. I didn't feel it when I bumped into him, but I wish I had."

"He very likely hid it inside his coat," Joe agreed. "Try not to think about it. There's nothing to be gained from wishing we did things differently. All we can do is to move forward from here. Keep in mind, the purpose of reviewing the video isn't to play Monday morning quarterback. It's to search for clues, hints as to who he is and where he might be now."

"I know." She understood where he was coming from and turned her attention back to the screen. "Okay, so he was probably standing in the bed of the truck. Then he jumped down when you turned to fire at him, slid in behind the wheel, and took off."

"That's the theory." Joe abruptly stood and paced. "They can test the soil in the truck bed, see if it matches a specific place, but I still think this guy has military or law enforcement background. That's the only thing that makes sense."

"Maybe he also worked construction," she suggested.

"It's possible." He raked his hand over his short hair. "I expected the BOLO to produce results by now."

"Rhy always says police work can be slow and tedious," she said, then immediately wished she hadn't mentioned her oldest brother. She didn't want to remind Joe that she was Rhy's youngest sibling. She needed him to see her as an individual—a woman—not an extension of his boss.

Not that he was likely to forget, she silently admitted.

He turned and crossed over to stare out the window. They were on the first floor this time, probably per Joe's request. For long moments, he didn't move. She crossed over to see what had captured his attention.

A blue glow from the Christmas lights that lined the

streets of Milwaukee could be seen in the distance. Ironically, the same lights she'd been entranced with when she'd accidentally bumped into the shooter.

"We're going to be fine, Joe." She sensed his despair. "We're safe here."

"Yeah." He turned from the window, his expression seemingly carved from granite. "I promised to look after you, Elly. The shooter shouldn't have been able to get close to you at all, much less this many times."

"We're alive because of you." She subtly tugged on the uncomfortable vest. She was wearing it mostly for his peace of mind.

"I can't lose—" He abruptly stopped himself, then moved back to the living room sofa. "Police work can be frustrating," he said instead.

Can't lose her? Is that what he'd been about to say? The thought warmed her heart. "What made you become a cop?" She sat on the sofa, taking care to put space between them. "Our dad was a cop; our mom was a nurse. Rhy wanted to follow in Dad's footsteps, and obviously, Tarin, Kyleigh, and even Brady did the same. My sister Alanna became a nurse, Colin a firefighter/paramedic. Quinn joined the Coast Guard, and Aiden the Army National Guard. Taking care of others seems to be a part of our DNA." *Genes we share with the Callahans*, she silently added.

He stared at his hands for a long moment before looking at her. "My sister and I grew up in an abusive household. My dad—let's just say he wasn't anything like yours. He was a mean drunk and never hesitated to lash out at us for every minor transgression."

She did her best not to look as horrified as she felt. "I'm so sorry, Joe. That's awful."

"My mom either couldn't or wouldn't leave. Not until the neighbor called the police during one of their physical fights, and they arrested him." Joe grimaced. "I often intervened, getting punched when I put myself between my dad and my mom or sister. That night, I suffered a broken arm and a few cracked ribs. There was no hiding what had happened. I had to be taken to Children's Memorial Hospital to be treated. To be honest, I was glad. And maybe a little angry with my mom for letting it come to that."

She knew there were many factors that contributed to a woman staying in an abusive relationship. Fear of the unknown, of not being able to find work or a safe place to stay. Fear of retribution. A lack of self-confidence and self-worth.

Yet it made her shiver to know Joe had sustained a broken arm and cracked ribs. She could easily imagine a younger version of him standing up to his father. She had to bite her lip to keep from crying out. She blocked the image and pulled herself together with an effort. "I'm glad your mom left him. I'm sure that was scary for her."

"Those first few months were rough. She almost went back to him, but the state stepped in and told her that she'd lose custody of us, sending me and Sarah into the foster care system if she did go back." He sighed. "I guess she finally decided to keep us rather than going back to him."

"It was the right thing to do, but not easy for her, I'm sure."

"Maybe, although I can't say I completely understand her reasoning."

"Do you still see her?"

"No. She ended up dying of cancer when I was twenty." He met her gaze. "My sister Sarah was eighteen. That was hard, but I would be lying if I didn't admit I was convinced that her death was partially her own fault. I feel certain that she didn't seek treatment earlier because she was still ingrained with that abusive mindset. That she wasn't worth the time and effort." He paused, then added, "I also think she blocked out the cancer symptoms the same way she blocked out the bruises and injures she sustained at my father's hand."

"I'm surprised you have any faith at all." The minute the words popped out, she wished she could call them back.

He looked away. "We went to church before Dad started drinking, then stopped. But when we were in one of the group homes, a pastor came to visit regularly. He talked about God and faith. But I still wasn't convinced, until I got to know Rhy." A faint smile tugged at the corner of his mouth. "Your brother is a man who lives his faith daily without trying to hide it."

"He does," she agreed. "And he made sure we continued attending church the way our parents taught us too."

"Obviously my parents doing the church thing didn't mean much." He shook his head. "I'm sure my dad only attended to put on a show for everyone else. As if to prove he wasn't a mean, abusive drunk."

"I'm sorry," she repeated helplessly. No child should have to go through what Joe and his sister, Sarah, had. She reached across the gap between them to rest her hand on his knee.

"You have nothing to apologize for." He shrugged as if he hadn't just bared his soul. He covered her hand with his, his palm warm to the touch. "You asked why I became a cop, and that was to help others. People in similar situations that we were in. It was good for me to be able to take action, just like the officers who responded to our house the night the neighbor called." He hesitated, then added, "Unfortunately, I've seen far worse cases of abuse than what Sarah and I suffered."

Her stomach rolled at the images that flashed in her brain. There was probably a good reason she hadn't made it through the police academy. She didn't have the physical or emotional strength that was needed to face what Joe and the other cops were confronted with each day.

"You're a great cop, Joe." She managed a smile despite the heaviness in her heart. "Rhy values you as a member of his team."

"We appreciate him too." He removed his hand as if worried Rhy might drop in at any moment to catch them together. She tried not to take his withdrawal personally. "It's late, time for you to get some sleep."

"Just me?" She didn't move from the sofa. "Pretty sure you need sleep too."

"Yeah." He stood and paced again, clearly on edge. This case was getting to him, and she didn't know how to reassure him she was fine. "Soon. I need to wait to see if Steele or any of the other team members find anything helpful."

"Joe." She uncurled from the sofa and rose. "I don't want you to stress about this. I love my life, but I'm not afraid to die."

"Don't say that." His tone was sharp. "You're not going to die."

"Like I said, I love my life. I'm looking forward to our Christmas family reunion with the Callahans." She took another step toward him. "But I also want to reassure you I'm at peace with the Lord."

He shook his head again. "We're not going down that path, okay? We're not."

It made her a little sad to realize how much he resisted

having faith in life after death. She reached for his hand. "Trust me, I'm with you one hundred percent. We're going to find this man, and you're going to throw him behind bars for the rest of his life."

He tugged her closer, his blue eyes holding hers. She eagerly stepped into his embrace, wrapping her arms around his waist. "I won't let anything happen to you, Elly." His words were muffled against her hair.

"I trust you."

He held her close for a long moment, then abruptly released her, stepping back and looking around the room, anywhere but at her. "Get some sleep. I—uh, need to make a call."

He turned away and hurried into his room as if Rhy himself was chasing him. And maybe he was. At least in Joe's mind.

She stood in the center of the room, feeling bereft. In that moment, it was clear to her that Joe would never act on their mutual attraction. That their one and only kiss was nothing but an aberration.

Joe would never allow a relationship to develop between them because of his dedication to his boss.

And there was nothing she could do to change his mind.

HE NEEDED out of this hotel room bad. Joe quietly closed the bedroom door behind him, then looked up at the ceiling as if seeking help from God.

Elly was messing with his mind in a way he'd never thought possible. He hadn't told anyone about the abuse he and Sarah had suffered. Yet one simple look from Elly had him blabbing about everything.

He was drawn to her in a way he hadn't experienced since—ever. Certainly not with Tina.

Pulling his phone from his pocket, he scrolled through his recent call list to call Rhy. Then he stopped himself.

What exactly would he say? Oh, by the way, Rhy, I need you to have someone else from the team to stay here with Elly because I desperately want to kiss her.

He snorted. Yeah, that would not go over well. He shouldn't be thinking of kissing Elly Finnegan in the first place. Something Rhy would no doubt point out in no uncertain terms.

Much less remembering the incredible kiss they'd already shared. And the warmth of her embrace.

See? He shoved his phone back into his pocket and began to pace again. This was exactly what Steele had warned him about. Keeping his mind on the game plan. Not allowing his personal feelings to interfere with their mission of finding and arresting this guy.

So why was he having so much trouble ignoring his attraction to her?

He didn't know but needed to figure it out and fast. Before he made another colossal mistake.

Besides, even if Rhy called him right now to tell him to hand Elly over to another member of the team, he wouldn't do it. Sure, the men and women he served with were highly trained professionals. They were the best of the best. He trusted them with his life on a regular basis.

But not with Elly's.

Okay, enough. Time to stop thinking about Elly and get to work. The quickest way out of this mess was to find the shooter.

Before the guy found Elly.

Taking a deep breath to calm himself, Joe opened the

bedroom door and stepped back into the living room. He'd hoped Elly would have taken his advice to get some rest, but she didn't.

"I'm going to keep searching social media pages of our victims." He sat down at the table and tapped the track screen to reengage the power.

"Can I help?" Elly asked.

"Not yet." He glanced over his shoulder, grateful she was still on the sofa. "I'll let you know if I find anyone matching your sketch. Besides, you should really get some sleep."

"I will when you do."

It was tempting to pretend to do just that to force her hand. But knowing Elly, she would hear him moving around and just join him anyway.

Turning his attention to the computer, he gave up on the skaters and went to the next victim he remembered. Not the eight-year-old boy, he couldn't imagine he was the intended victim. Kyle? No, he didn't have social media.

There was another young couple who'd been hit. He pulled up the list of victims, found the woman's name, and typed it into the search engine. Before he could do anything more, his phone rang.

He expected the call to be from Rhy or one of Elly's other siblings, but he didn't recognize the number on the screen. He debated sending the call to voice mail, expecting a robo call letting him know his warranty is up, but given the circumstances, he answered it. "Kingsley."

"Why haven't you found him?" The shrill voice in his ear had him pulling the phone away with a wince.

"Ah, ma'am? Who are you?" He hadn't recognized the voice, so he didn't think this was Gabrielle's or Henry's mother.

"Kyle's widow!" Her tone increased in volume. "I demand to know what you're doing to find the man who shot my husband!"

He remembered how Rhy had mentioned getting an irate phone call from Kyle's wife, Eloise. Rhy could have warned him that he'd given Kyle's widow his number. Elly must have been able to hear the woman, too, as she came over to sit beside him.

"We're doing everything possible," he said in a calm, reassuring tone. "I promise, we will find him."

"When?" She sounded slightly less antagonistic. "I don't understand what's taking so long. It's been over twenty-four hours."

"I know. We have a sketch of our perp circulating through every precinct in the city, and his face has been put out on all the news stations. He won't be able to hide for long."

"You have to find him!" Her voice rose again in agitation. "You owe Kyle that much, don't you?"

"Yes, of course." He wondered if that was part of the reason for Eloise acting out. Normally, when an officer was taken from them, they visited the widow. Providing support through a difficult time.

They hadn't done that, their priority being to find this guy before he opened fire on other innocent people again. "Do you need anything? Is there something I can do for you?"

"Just find Kyle's killer!" With that, she disconnected from the call.

He sat in silence for a long moment.

"She's grieving," Elly said. "If you like, I can try to talk to her once we have Kyle's killer in custody. Maybe she needs another woman to talk to."

"Maybe." Logically, he knew everyone handled grief differently. And this was a highly unusual circumstance. "I need to let Assistant Chief Michaels know. A visit from the upper brass may be in order."

"That's a good idea," Elly agreed. "She's probably feeling lost amidst the media attention."

The media attention was to help find this guy, but he let it go. He made the call to Assistant Chief Michaels. "Do you have something, Kingsley?" he asked.

He wished he did. "No, sir. Nothing concrete. I think the crime scene techs have been over the truck but haven't found any prints or DNA."

"Then why are you calling?" Michaels sounded irritated.

"I just got off the phone with Eloise Malaki, Kyle's widow. She's pretty upset, and I was thinking she may need a visit from you, or the chief of police, or even the mayor. I think she feels forgotten in this."

"Yeah, you're right." Michaels sounded tired. "I usually count on Finnegan to navigate this stuff. But I know he's taking well deserved vacation time. And we haven't followed our usual protocol either. I'll make an appointment to see her first thing tomorrow."

"Thank you, sir." It was telling how their assistant chief depended on Rhy to keep things moving. Not that he planned to point that out to the older guy. He doubted Michaels would appreciate the comparison. He tucked his phone back into his pocket, hoping the assistant chief could smooth things over with Eloise Malaki.

As a cop, he'd seen all sorts of inappropriate angry outbursts. Many aimed at the cops either because they were there or because they hadn't done enough.

He wasn't sure why he was taking Eloise's anger so

personally. But he was irked that she didn't believe they were doing everything in their power to get the guy who'd callously killed a cop. Along with nine other victims.

"Is Kyle on social media?" Elly asked, breaking into his thoughts.

He glanced at her, wishing she wasn't so close. "No, none of us are active on any of those sites. But you bring up a good point. It's possible Eloise is."

"Can't hurt to check."

He did so, somewhat surprised to find she indeed had one. "Here she is."

Elly leaned closer. "She's beautiful."

"Yeah. Kyle always mentioned how she won the Miss Wisconsin pageant a few years back." He poked around on the page. "I see lots of sympathy comments here," he said, scrolling through them. "Nothing unusual about that. But I can't see all her posts because she has privacy settings in place. I'm glad she took that much of a precaution." Maybe being a former Miss Wisconsin had taught her there were creeps out in the world.

More than one, he silently amended.

"You know, some people like to stay in touch with friends or family," Elly said with a hint of defensiveness. "It's not all about posting pictures of your recent meal at a nice restaurant or selfies on vacation."

He let out a laugh. "I truly don't get it. Especially the part where people tell the entire world they're on vacation, announcing to the world their house is empty. That's an open invitation to all criminals. But then again, in my line of work, I've seen social media used to trick women and kids into being trafficked."

"That's horrifying." Elly shook her head. "I'm glad Rhy always made us stay off those sites."

"He's like a father to you," He hoped that saying the words out loud would remind him to keep his distance.

"He held the family together and has always been supportive of me and the twins as we were the youngest of the bunch. But no, Joe, he never tried to take over the role of my father." She held his gaze steadily. "Our parents died; he made sure we remembered them. And even as he was guiding us, he reminded us that this was what our parents would have wanted."

He didn't believe that, mostly because Rhy had warned him off the way a father would, but he let it go. Just because Elly didn't see Rhy as a father figure didn't mean her brother hadn't taken on that role. Quite the opposite.

Joe was firmly convinced Rhy had.

He turned back to the computer, deciding to move on. Then he had an idea. He pulled out his phone again and sent Assistant Chief Michaels a text, asking him to check with Eloise for her permission to review all her social media posts.

Michaels responded with a brief, "Okay."

It wasn't a priority now, but he felt the need to check off all the boxes.

To search every single victim for a connection, no matter how remote, to the shooter.

"Maybe we should go back to the skaters' profiles," Elly mused. "They must have been the main target."

"Sure." He did as she'd asked, even though he desperately wished she'd try to get some sleep. Or go anywhere that was farther away from him.

Her scent was driving him crazy.

They were both silent as he made his way through their social media pages. Although several times he had to go through them twice.

Yeah, this wasn't working. He needed to put an end to this forced togetherness for a while. He needed time to regroup. And maybe by morning the shooter will have been picked up by one of the thousands of cops searching for him.

"It's no use, I don't see anything new." He made a show of glancing at his watch. "It's getting late. We need to get some sleep."

"I'm too wired to sleep."

He hesitated, wondering if she was afraid of having more nightmares. But then she leaned against him, resting her head on his shoulder.

"I—uh," he floundered, trying to come up with an excuse. "Need a break." Gently disentangling himself from her, he rose and moved away from the computer.

She sighed loudly, without bothering to hide her exasperation. "Okay, okay. I'll take the hint and leave you alone."

He hadn't meant to hurt her, but he would be much better off if she would leave. At least for a while. He stood awkwardly for a moment, debating taking the computer into his room and shutting the door.

Elly rose and walked over to the window, the one he'd stared out earlier.

"No. You know what?" She abruptly spun away from the window, heading toward him. "It's not okay . . ."

The sharp crack of gunfire had him instinctively lunging toward her, taking her down to the ground like a linebacker sacking the quarterback. He heard the muted sound of a slug embedding itself in the sofa that was right next to them, followed by yet another retort of gunfire. "Stay down!" he shouted hoarsely.

He covered her body with his, mentally braced for the sharp, painful impact of being struck by a bullet.

CHAPTER TEN

Squashed between the unyielding floor and Joe's hard body, Elly couldn't scream. Could barely breathe as she struggled to comprehend how the shooter had found her.

Again!

"Officer needs assistance! Gunfire at the City Central Hotel!" Joe's tense tone broke into her thoughts. He'd managed to maintain the presence of mind to call 911.

She tried to lift her head but couldn't. Joe was stretched out on top of her.

"Stay down!" His curt voice left no room for argument.

"Maybe we should crawl to the bedroom." She didn't want Joe to be hit by gunfire either. And the way he was protecting her left him vulnerable.

"I need backup." Joe was still talking into his phone, although she didn't think he was still on with the 911 dispatcher. "Shooter on the south side of the building."

It took a moment for her to recognize Steele's voice responding, "Be there in five."

The news that Steele was close helped calm her racing nerves. Yet she needed to breathe. "Up," she croaked.

As if finally understanding her dilemma, Joe lifted himself up onto his elbows, taking the brunt of his weight off her. "Stay down," he repeated. "He could still be out there, and I don't want to give him another target."

It was both humbling and horrifying the way Joe put his life on the line for her. Well, probably more so for Rhy than for her. "I'd rather get out of here."

"Not yet." Joe didn't move. "Steele will be here soon."

She didn't like it but decided to let it go. He'd promised her brother to watch over her and would die to keep that vow. All she could do was to put her faith in God and in the members of Rhy's tactical team.

Please, Lord Jesus, keep us all safe in Your care!

As the seconds ticked by with agonizing slowness, she understood these relentless attacks against her wouldn't stop until she was dead, or the shooter was arrested.

And the way things were going, she felt certain the first would happen before the second.

In that moment, she made a silent promise to kiss Joe again before she was taken from this earth to be home with Jesus.

Surely, he wouldn't deny her that much.

"Joe?" Steele pounded on the door. "Are you okay?"

"Yeah." Joe crawled over her to cross the room. At the door, he stood in a crouch and let Steele in. "Thanks for coming."

"We need to get you both out of here." Steele's tone was just as grim as Joe's. "Let's move."

"Anyone out there searching for the shooter?" Joe asked as he grabbed the computer, tucked it under his arm, then crossed over to help her up.

"Brock, Grayson, and Raelyn." Steele glanced at her. "Where's your coat?"

"I'll get it." Joe thrust the computer at his teammate. "Keep her close."

Swallowing hard, she huddled beside Steele. "I don't understand how this happened."

"It shouldn't have." Steele scowled. Before he could say anything more, Joe returned with her winter coat.

Her hands trembled as she pulled it on. The extra layer of fabric didn't offer any additional warmth. The temperature in the room wasn't the problem.

It was the situation that had chilled her to the bone. Leaving her to bleakly wonder if she'd ever be warm again.

"We're taking the side exit." Steele led the way down the hall.

Joe nudged her forward so that she was between the two men. Her coat barely stretched over the extra layer of the vest. She supposed it was a good thing she'd been wearing it, and Joe, too, for that matter. Yet from the hole in the window, she could tell the shooter had been aiming for her head.

If she hadn't gotten so frustrated with Joe's attempt to keep her at arm's length that she'd abruptly turned away from the window at that exact moment, she'd be dead.

She stumbled, but Joe caught her from behind. "Almost there," he said encouragingly.

Managing to stay on her feet, she followed Steele outside. The SUV was parked close to the building. Steele stood near the back passenger door and helped her in.

Joe ran around to get into the passenger seat as Steele dropped the computer on the floorboard and slid behind the wheel. Seconds later, they were careening out of the parking lot and out onto the road.

For long moments, no one spoke. She stared at Joe's

profile, then abruptly frowned when she saw something dark along the side of his neck.

Was that blood?

"Joe, are you hit?" Amazingly, she didn't feel sick or faint as she leaned forward to get a better look. "You're bleeding."

"I'm fine." He reached up to touch the area. "It's a scratch."

"We need to take care of that." She was proud of the steadiness of her tone.

"Later." Joe dismissed her concern. "It's more important to find a safe house."

"I don't understand how the City Central Hotel became compromised," Steele said with obvious frustration. "I made sure I wasn't followed."

"We may have underestimated this guy," Joe said with a sigh. "I've suspected military and/or law enforcement background. It could be he has decent access to intel."

"This shouldn't have happened." Steele lightly pounded his fist on the steering wheel. "Rhy is going to flip out."

"Don't tell him," Elly said. When Steele's incredulous gaze met hers in the rearview mirror, she added, "Not yet. Let's stay focused on our next steps."

"Elly's right," Joe said. "I'll call Brady. We need a safe house."

"You know Rhy's going to hear about it sooner rather than later," Steele muttered. "Better to call him first."

"I'll do it." Elly patted her pockets, relieved to find the disposable phone in her coat pocket. She entered Rhy's number.

He answered on the second ring. "Elly? Are you okay?"

"Yes, I'm with Joe and Steele. But you should know that

the window of our hotel suite at the City Central Hotel was hit by gunfire. We're all fine, though," she added for extra emphasis.

"What in the world is going on?" Rhy demanded. "I want to talk to Joe."

"He's reaching out to Brady for a safe house," she said calmly. "That's why I'm calling you."

"This is unbelievable," Rhy said, still sounding upset. "I don't understand why this perp isn't in custody by now."

"I wish he was too, but it sounds like several of the team members are out searching the area around the hotel." She wasn't sure what else to say to reassure her brother. "We're doing everything we can, Rhy."

"I know, I know." She could imagine her brother running his hands through his short blond hair. "I'd really like to talk to Joe."

She sighed. "Okay, hang on."

Joe finished his call with Brady, then reached for her phone. "I'm here." There was a pause, then, "I wish I could tell you how this happened, but I don't know. We've been safe there for the past sixteen hours."

Difficult to comprehend that this nightmare had only started Saturday evening. It seemed like she had been on the run from this guy for days instead of hours.

"I understand. Brady has arranged for an FBI safe house. We're heading there now and will be in touch later." Joe ended the call and handed the phone back to her. "Rhy is obviously upset, but he's glad we're getting a safe house from Brady."

"I feel responsible," Steele said in a low tone. "I watched for a tail, but maybe I missed something."

"This guy has a scope, maybe even a set of binocs," Joe said. "Brady is going to meet us at the FBI offices where we can swap rides. The safe house he's arranging for us is only three miles away from that location."

"I'm surprised the FBI is giving us a safe house."

"I'm not." Joe glanced back at her. "For one thing, you're an FBI agent's sister. For another, the feds are treating this guy as a domestic terrorist."

Thinking of the man she'd bumped into as a terrorist made her shiver. Yet she knew Joe was right. After killing so many innocent people, every law enforcement agency in the state wanted him apprehended.

"I guess the good news is that he's only targeting me, not other innocent victims."

"That's hardly good news," Steele said in a dry tone. "Having him in custody would be good news."

She shrugged. "Better me than taking out more innocent lives at another public event." She abruptly straightened. "Wait a minute, what about the Milwaukee Performing Arts Center? They're featuring live performances of the Christmas Carol every Thursday through Sunday from now until Christmas. What if we're wrong about him not looking to take more innocent lives? What if he's just buying time until the next event?"

Steele and Joe exchanged a look. "I've been wondering if there shouldn't be a shelter in place order, but that's not my call to make," Joe said. "Truth is, he's been following you. If he'd wanted to take out a bunch of visitors at the theater, he could have done that by now. They had a matinee performance today and another show tonight. But he showed up at the hotel instead."

She wasn't convinced. In some ways she hoped this guy was only interested in her.

They arrived at the FBI offices faster than she'd

expected. Seeing Brady in his SUV waiting for them eased some of the knots in her stomach.

When Steele pulled up next to him, Brady and Joe lowered their respective windows.

"Ready to jump in?" Brady asked.

"Let's do it," Joe agreed.

Both Joe and Steele got out first, then crowded around her until she was situated in the back of Brady's car. Joe crawled in beside her, leaving Steele to take the front passenger seat.

"You're going to leave the other SUV here?" she asked.

"For now." Brady met her gaze in the rearview. "Marc Callahan will get us another rental in the morning."

"Callahan?" Steele asked.

"Our cousin," Brady and Elly said at the same time. If the situation wasn't so dire, she'd have laughed.

The safe house was a nondescript tan brick home located on a half acre of land. A few minutes later, they were all crowded in the kitchen.

"You still think this is related to the ice skaters?" Brady asked.

Joe lifted his hands. "The only thing I know for sure is that this guy is determined to kill Elly. And that's not typical behavior from an active shooter."

"True," Brady admitted. "Ian has still been searching for the missing kid. I hope to have him switched over to working on the facial recognition sometime tomorrow. There's a lead that Callahan is following up on related to the kid. If he's found, that will free up more resources."

Elly was secretly glad that a missing child had taken priority. God had kept her and Joe safe so far.

She felt certain the local police and the FBI would have the shooter in custody very soon.

The guys huddled together at the kitchen table, discussing theories. Elly did her best to pay attention, but her mind kept replaying those moments at the City Central Hotel. She'd been about to confront Joe about her feelings, but the shooter firing through the window, nearly killing her and Joe, had put an end to that plan.

She couldn't help feeling as if she was living on borrowed time. There wasn't a single doubt in her mind that this guy would try again.

Having faith in God, and in Joe and the rest of the team, didn't mean she wasn't prepared for the possibility of being hurt.

Or worse.

All she needed was a few minutes alone with Joe. She wanted to let him know how she felt before it was too late.

"I should take a look at your cut," she said, interrupting them.

Three pairs of eyes looked at her in surprise. Then Brady must have noticed the dried blood on Joe's neck.

"It's no big deal," Joe said. "We have more important issues to discuss."

"Fine. You talk while I bandage." She stood and walked through the kitchen and living room to find the bathroom. There she found soap and towels but no bandages.

"You want me to get Alanna's first aid kit?" Brady asked.

Joe scoffed. "You mean that suitcase disguised as a first aid kit? That's not necessary." He rose from the table. "I'll take care of it myself."

Swallowing a wave of annoyance, she spun on her heel and followed him to the bathroom. "Here." She thrust the soap and towels at him. "I guess you don't need me."

"Elly, wait." Joe caught her arm. "Are you okay? You seem upset."

She bit back a sarcastic reply. "There isn't much I can do to help, but I am an EMT. First aid is what I do."

"Ah, okay. But I thought you didn't like blood."

"I got over it." She gestured to the commode, so he sat down. "Responding to the injured victims at the parade put an end to that." It wasn't entirely true. If she imagined the bloody scene of the ice skaters or the pool of blood running down from Kyle's body, the nausea returned. But the bloody area on Joe's neck didn't bother her. It was minimal in the big scheme of things.

It was all about perspective.

"Okay, then." He took off his sweatshirt, revealing the vest he wore beneath. "Have at it."

She cleaned the wound with soap and water, relieved to find he was right about the injury not being serious. "I'd appreciate if you didn't mention my irrational fears to my siblings."

"Of course not," Joe quickly assured her.

She nodded and patted the skin around the laceration with a dry towel. "It wouldn't hurt to put antibiotic ointment on this."

"Later." He shrugged back into his shirt. "Thanks."

She stood for a moment, her head down.

"Hey. It's going to be okay." Joe stood and wrapped one arm around her shoulders.

She leaned against him, trying to find the words to explain her feelings. Then she looked up at him. "I need one more thing from you."

He nodded. "Sure. Name it."

"This." She lifted onto her tiptoes and kissed him.

It only took a second for Joe to respond to her kiss, the way she'd hoped he would. This kiss even better than the last one. He hauled her closer, angling his mouth over hers in a way that sent shock waves through her body down to the soles of her feet.

Surely Joe couldn't kiss her like that if he was completely indifferent to her.

The sound of a throat clearing had Joe breaking off their embrace and stumbling backward as if he couldn't get away from her fast enough.

"What's going on?" Brady asked.

She glared at her brother, but Joe lifted his hands. "Elly was upset. I—didn't mean, I only wanted to offer comfort . . ."

His words washed over her like an ice-cold shower. He didn't care about her, not in the way she'd thought.

No, it was clear that Joe wasn't going to accept her love, no matter how much she wanted him to.

JOE WAS CAUGHT COMPLETELY off guard by Elly's kiss. He hadn't expected her to do such a thing when her brother Brady was nearby.

"We need to figure out a game plan," Brady said, eyeing him intensely.

"I know." He couldn't bear to meet Elly's gaze. He hated feeling like he was a kid with his hand caught in the cookie jar.

Although the one time he'd tried to snatch a cookie, his dad had slapped him halfway across the room. He supposed he should be relieved Brady hadn't done that considering the way he'd practically devoured his younger sister.

Nothing like playing with fire, he thought as he followed Brady back to the kitchen. He noticed Elly stayed behind, and it took all his willpower not to go back to make sure she was okay.

Seriously, he needed to get a grip. He couldn't keep kissing Elly or letting her kiss him either. This absolutely couldn't happen again.

"I just got a call from Brock," Steele said. "They think they found the shooter's location, but of course, there's no sign of him now."

"How does he keep getting away?" Joe asked.

"Good question." Brady frowned. "Your theory that this guy is either in law enforcement or the military is a good one. I'll put a call into Heath Strauss. He may be able to help provide some intel on recent military discharges."

"Who?" Joe scowled. "I've never heard of the guy."

"He's a military investigator. We worked with him back when Aiden was having trouble keeping a widow and her young daughter safe." Brady arched a brow. "Aiden and Shelby are engaged now too. They're getting married next month."

Was that some sort of subtle dig? Did Brady expect Joe to propose now that he'd kissed Elly?

The idea was more intriguing than annoying. He quickly averted his thoughts to the immediate threat of the gunman.

"Okay, give Strauss a call. Obviously, we can use all the help we can get." Joe turned back to Steele. "Can you think of any reason why a former cop or military dude would do this? The motive is what keeps tripping me up."

"No," Steele said. "It doesn't make sense."

"Other than it must be personal," Brady interjected. "No way is this a simple act of violence to make a statement. We've had profilers working on these types of incidents. As you've said all along, this one doesn't fit the typical pattern.

Most shootings are racially or religiously motivated, or they're young men angry at the group of people they've targeted, like terminated employees or being bullied at a school." He shook his head and sighed. "There is more going on here than we understand."

"Yeah." Joe glanced around the interior of the house. "It's late; we need to get some sleep. But it may be helpful to have Steele stay the night."

"I can sleep on the sofa," Brady offered.

"It's better if I plan to take a defensive position outside," Steele said. "It seems this guy doesn't get that close, but maybe if I'm stationed near the perimeter, I'll find him before he can take another shot at Elly."

"He shouldn't know about this place at all," Joe protested.

"Yeah, like the City Central Hotel," Steele shot back.

His teammate was right. He didn't like the idea of his buddy staying outside in the cold, though. "Too bad we don't have another property nearby that we can use."

"Hang on." Brady worked his phone for a few minutes. "Okay, there is a house across the street that you can use."

"How many safe houses do you have?" Joe couldn't hide his surprise. Granted, his experience with working alongside the feds was limited.

Brady shrugged. "We didn't have much to offer until recently. I put up a stink after the last incident with Aiden and Shelby. MPD has had better safe houses than we have. For once, Donovan, our special agent in charge of the Milwaukee field office, agreed with me. Shortly after that, these two properties were purchased by the bureau from the bank during foreclosure. They're not perfect, but they'll do."

"I like it." Steele rose. "It's good to have two properties

close together to help keep an eye on things. I wouldn't mind if the shooter decided to use the roof of the house I'll be staying in to aim at this one."

"That would be nice," Brady drawled. "But don't count on it."

Steele shrugged. "I can hope, right? I'll head over there now and have Brock or one of the others on the team come relieve me in a few hours."

Joe knew that was the right thing to do, everyone on the team was determined to keep Elly safe, and nobody could stay awake and alert for hours on end. Sleep was critical to staying sharp.

But he also hated taking resources from tracking the shooter. He tried to console himself there was a BOLO for this guy, which meant every cop in a fifty-mile radius should be looking for him.

Should, in fact, have found him already.

"Yeah, okay," he reluctantly agreed. "We can make that work for tonight."

Armed with the key code information, Steele shrugged into his leather jacket and left. Brady headed into the living room.

Joe stood, knowing he owed the Finnegan sibling an apology. "I—didn't mean to kiss Elly."

Brady arched a brow as he stretched out on the sofa. "Didn't see a gun pointed at your head."

"No." He dropped into the chair next to the couch, glancing toward the bedrooms. "You're right."

Brady didn't respond right away. Finally, he said, "Elly's going to be twenty-five the first week in January. I don't think you're the first guy she's kissed, Joe."

He tried not to squirm in his seat. Why did that thought bother him? It wasn't as if he hadn't had girlfriends before.

Like Tina. "I know that. I'm not saying this correctly. I care about Elly, very much. I wouldn't kiss her if I didn't. But I understand this isn't the time or the place for that. Rhy has put his trust in me to keep her safe."

"Ah." Brady nodded. "I see."

Did he? Joe wished he did. He pressed on. "I would never hurt Elly. She's going through a rough time. I never meant for our brief hug to spiral out of control."

Brady held his gaze for a long moment. "Yes, she is going through a hard time. None of us are happy to know she's been targeted by this guy. But I am going to hold you to that promise, Kingsley."

Joe nodded in understanding. "I will gladly protect her with my life if necessary."

"That wasn't the promise I meant," Brady said with a crooked smile. "As a cop, you would always protect an innocent person with your life. It's the nature of the career we've chosen. Your relationship is between the two of you. But know this, Elly has a tender heart. I won't be happy if you hurt her."

"I won't." Even as he said the words, he knew he already had hurt her by pulling away from their kiss so abruptly.

It was reassuring that Brady hadn't gone all big brother on him. And he couldn't help wondering how Rhy would have acted if he'd been the one to interrupt their kiss instead of Brady.

Maybe once they had this perp in custody, he'd have to talk to Rhy to explain how much he cared for Elly.

Would his boss let him date his younger sister? There was only one way to find out.

CHAPTER ELEVEN

Elly didn't sleep well. First because of Joe's withdrawal after the most incredible kiss of her entire life, and then because she'd woken up with another nightmare about the shooting. She had a feeling the nightmares weren't going to end anytime soon. Possibly once they had the shooter in custody, but even then, she knew soldiers and cops could be haunted by PTSD for months to years after a terrible event.

Thankfully, she'd felt slightly better by morning. And in the cold light of day, she'd decided to move on from her infatuation with Joe. Her older siblings had all found love when they'd least expected it. Joe had always treated her kindly but like a younger sister. Someone to look out for.

Not as a woman he wanted to be in a relationship with.

Time for her to let him go. Forcing the issue wouldn't work. She needed to put her faith in God to find the man who was right for her. One who was as attracted to her as she was to him. One that wanted to be with her, rather than being ordered to stay close by her older brother.

It would take time for her to recover from the horror of the Christmas parade tragedy. It hurt her heart to know so many innocent people had died. Especially the beautiful figure skater, Gabrielle. On the bright side, blood no longer made her feel like passing out. Maybe there was still a bit of nausea, but nothing compared to what she'd experienced in the past. It felt good to know her career as an EMT might work out after all. Thankfully, she'd never mentioned her doubts to her older sibs.

She might even check into becoming a paramedic. Something to think about in January.

She quickly showered and dressed. She spent a few extra minutes blow-drying her hair to make herself feel better. Not to show Joe what he was missing.

Okay, maybe a little to show Joe what he was missing.

Enough. She shook off the gloom and opened the bedroom door. Joe and Brady were already seated at the small table, both with cups of coffee nearby. They were speaking in whispers so as not to wake her.

"Good morning." She injected cheerfulness into her tone.

"Hey, El," Brady said. "How did you sleep?"

"Great." It wasn't true, but there was no point in dwelling on the nightmares.

"Would you like coffee?" Joe jumped up from the table. "I just made a fresh pot."

"Sure." Keeping her expression casual, she walked over. "What are you working on?"

"More digging into the victim's backgrounds." Brady scrubbed his hands over his face. Her brother looked tired, and she knew he'd rather be home with his wife, Grace, and son, Caleb.

"Here you go." Joe brought her coffee with cream and sugar, the way she liked it.

"Thanks." She accepted the cup and took a sip. These

were the small things that made it difficult to ignore her attraction to him. "I'd like to help."

"With what?" Joe looked confused.

"This." She waved at the computer. "The sooner we find this guy, the faster our lives can get back to normal."

Joe and Brady exchanged a look. She knew what they were thinking.

"I may not be a cop, but I'm not stupid. And I'm the one who saw this guy up close."

"Neither of us thinks you're stupid," Brady protested. "And we're grateful to have you as our key witness. But there is only one computer. Better to let us do the digging to come up with possible suspects for you to identify."

"I caught a glimpse of him too," Joe said. "I can narrow our search down to those who are the most likely candidates to be our guy."

She suppressed a sigh. "Fine. But what am I supposed to do while you guys hover around the computer?"

"Ah, Steele picked up some groceries for us. There's plenty of breakfast food if you're hungry," Joe suggested.

"Okay. That works. Do I need to make something for him too?"

"No, Steele needs to stay put." Brady met her gaze. "He can cook his own meals, sis."

She nodded in understanding. To be honest, she didn't mind cooking meals for the guys. She'd been pitching in to help Devon and Rhy after they brought Colleen home. She opened the fridge and reviewed her options.

She knew what Brady would want, so she turned to Joe. "What would you like?"

"Whatever is easiest for you," Joe said.

"Having you tell me what you'd like is what is easiest for me." She couldn't hide her exasperation.

"Okay, eggs over easy with bacon and toast?" He made it sound like a question.

"Got it." She pulled items out of the fridge and went to work. The television was on in the living room, but the sound was muted. She imagined the guys had watched it on silent mode while she slept in.

Or tried to.

From what she could tell, the news anchor was regurgitating the same information over and over again, the way they often did to fill airtime. Then a list of victims flashed on the screen.

She audibly gasped. "Wait! There are twelve victims now?"

Joe glanced over. "Last I heard there were eleven."

"Twelve." She scanned the names. Kyle's name was on there, along with others that she didn't recognize. But then she winced when she saw a woman named Lisa Beaumont. She remembered the way Dan had cradled his wife in his arms while she asked why this was happening.

And of course, Henry Watkins the male figure skater was also on the list. That wasn't as surprising, he'd been the second victim, shot right after Gabrielle.

But Lisa? It seemed inconceivable to learn the young woman had died.

She closed her eyes for a moment, bracing her hands on the counter for support, trying to erase the images from her mind. Her name could have been on the list. Even worse, Joe's name could have been there instead of Kyle's.

God was watching over her. And over Joe too. She needed to try to stay focused on the positive side of things rather than wallowing in the negative. Yet that was also easier said than done.

When she felt a warm hand on her shoulder, she glanced up, expecting to see Brady.

But it was Joe standing there, eyeing her with concern. "Are you okay?"

She shook her head, gesturing at the screen. "A woman named Lisa died. The last time I saw her, she was being cradled in her husband's arms. I thought she would be okay. I—wasn't expecting so see her name on the list of victims."

"I'm sorry." Joe's voice was low and husky.

He needed to stop being so nice to her, or she'd never figure out how to get over him. She drew in a deep breath, then let it out slowly. "It's okay. The shooter is responsible for this. I'll be fine."

He didn't move his hand, his gaze holding hers. "We're going to find him."

"I know." She turned her attention back to the task of making breakfast. Maybe watching the news hadn't been such a good idea.

Joe's hand lingered for a moment before he pulled away. "You need any help?"

"No. I can do it." Her appetite was gone. The nausea was back, but it wasn't because of seeing blood. No, this time it was simply the loss of innocent lives that made her sick to her stomach.

She began making bacon. Then paused and glanced back at the guys. "Maybe you should dig deeper into Henry's background from a personal perspective, not just as a skater. It could be that the shooter had intended him to die all along, and maybe he was even the real target."

A flash of admiration brightened Joe's blue eyes. "You could be onto something. We thought Gabrielle was the first target, but the two of them were so close together, it could be that Henry was really taken out first."

Her cheeks warmed, and she silently bemoaned her red hair and fair skin. A simple compliment from Joe shouldn't cause her to blush like this.

When the bacon was almost finished, she made the eggs and toast. It didn't take that long for her to finish the meal. When she carried the plate of bacon to the table, Joe grinned.

"Yum." He rose to help her bring their plates to the table. "This all looks great, Elly."

"Thanks." His kind words warmed her heart.

When Brady opened his mouth, she quickly spoke up. "I'd like to say grace, Brady, if you don't mind."

He looked surprised. Usually the older siblings took on the role of praying before their meals. "Sure."

Joe took her hand, causing her to momentarily lose her train of thought. Then she pulled herself together. "Lord Jesus, we thank You for this food we are about to eat. We ask that You comfort the victim's families, especially Dan who recently lost his wife, Lisa during their time of grief. And we ask You to continue guiding us to the truth so that we may find this guy before he hurts anyone else. Amen."

"Amen," Joe echoed.

"Amen. That was great, sis," Brady said.

When Joe released her hand, it took all her willpower not to hold on tight. He was a pillar of strength, but she couldn't keep leaning on him for support. She needed to stand on her own two feet.

Elly picked up her fork and forced herself to eat. Considering the events over the past thirty-six hours, it would be smart to eat while they had the chance. If something happened here at the safe house, they may need to leave at a moment's notice.

Brady's cell phone rang, breaking the silence. He

glanced at the screen, wiped his mouth with a napkin, and stood to answer it. He moved away from their table to other side of the room. "I hope you're calling with good news, Marc."

She wished she could hear the other side of the conversation. Joe was silent beside her, focused on eating. She worked hard to keep from watching him.

"You have good instincts," Joe said.

His comment seemed to come out of the blue. "What do you mean?"

He shrugged. "From the very beginning of this nightmare, you've acted on your instincts. Running out to save victims, shouting at me to duck as the shooter took aim, and even now as we investigate the case in more detail." He paused, then added, "I'm impressed."

She tried not to gape. She impressed him? He was the tactical expert, the guy on the team that Rhy leaned on the most. She was about as far from a cop as anyone could get.

"I, um, thanks." She took another bite of her eggs. "I appreciate you saying that."

"I'm not just saying it," Joe protested. "It's true."

She wondered if he was saying these things to make up for breaking off their kiss so abruptly. If so, it wasn't necessary. She could understand that liking someone as a friend was different from falling in love.

But before she could say anything more, Brady's voice intruded on her thoughts.

"That's great, Marc. Send it to my personal email. We'll start going through the list ASAP."

"What list?" Elly looked up at her brother as he returned to his seat.

"The list of terminated Milwaukee cops." Brady's expression reflected satisfaction. "We had to push hard to get that information, considering we don't have any proof this guy is actually a cop."

"Glad to hear it," Joe said. "That gives us another angle to work."

"You think he's a disgruntled cop?" Elly had a hard time imagining the man she'd bumped into as a police officer. Then again, she was using her brothers Rhy and Tarin as role models.

And this guy was the antithesis of her brothers.

She finished her meal and sipped coffee while Joe and Brady continued eating. When they were done, she stood and stacked their dirty dishes together.

Joe jumped to his feet. "We should wash them since you cooked."

"No, you have work to do." She smiled at his willingness to chip in. "Trust me, this will help keep me busy for a while. I'm going a little stir-crazy here."

Joe searched her gaze for a moment, then dropped back into his seat. After she'd washed and dried the dishes, she moved back to the kitchen table.

"Are you sure there isn't something I can do?" She hated feeling helpless.

"Give us some time to pull some of these photos together." Joe gestured to the computer. "When we have a few viable suspects, you can review them with us."

"Okay." Patience is a virtue, she reminded herself. She dropped back onto the sofa and rested her head back on the cushion, staring at the ceiling.

She ended up closing her eyes and reviewing the tasks she still needed to do for the Callahan and Finnegan Christmas family reunion. She'd originally planned on renting a hall, but Rhy talked her into having the gathering at the homestead. He agreed to bring in a large canvas tent for the backyard, along with four propane patio heaters.

She hoped the families would mix and mingle, especially the spouses. Many of the cousins had met and worked together over the past year, even before she and Maddy had uncovered the DNA connection.

"Elly?" Joe's voice broke into her thoughts.

"Yes?" She opened her eyes, flushing when she realized she may have dozed a bit. "Do you have a list of possible suspects?"

"We do." Joe's smile made her toes tingle. "We culled the list to focus on white males in a certain age group, which helped narrow it down to eight men who fit the criteria. We're interested in your thoughts."

"Okay." She rose and stretched, then quickly crossed the room. Joe pulled out a chair, and she dropped down beside him. On the computer screen, she saw eight solemn faces staring back at her.

She almost immediately shook her head. The guy she'd bumped into wasn't one of these eight.

"Hold on, Elly," Joe cautioned. "Take your time."

This was police work, she reminded herself. She needed to be absolutely sure that the man she'd seen moments before the Christmas parade began wasn't there.

Taking one at a time, she tried to place the cop on the screen with the man with the cold, dead eyes wearing a long coat. Her gaze lingered on one face that had some similarities. But she didn't think he was the man she'd seen.

"I'm sorry," she said on a sigh. "This man here"—she tapped on the one photograph—"is close. But I don't think he's our guy."

"His name is Peter Colton, and he was terminated for use of excessive force," Brady said. "He was also described as a loner by those who knew him. He fits the general description you gave, Elly. And he's not that far off from your sketch either."

A wave of doubt hit hard. Was this the same man? Had she made a mistake with the sketch? Not getting it quite right?

Lord help her, she didn't know.

JOE COULD TELL Elly was struggling to match Peter Colton with the gunman in her mind. This cop was the only one who'd come close to fitting the profile.

But he wasn't an exact match to her sketch. He had only gotten a glimpse, he had trouble believing they were one and the same either. Sure, the guy's background was interesting. But that alone wasn't enough to accuse the guy of committing multiple murders as a domestic terrorist.

"He's similar in some ways," Elly said. "But I can't mesh this man with the one I saw. The description I gave Bethany as we worked on the sketch is imprinted in my mind. The minute Bethany finished the drawing, I knew she'd nailed it."

"You were under a lot of stress, El," Brady said gently.

"I know, but I also locked eyes with the gunman." She lifted her chin, meeting her brother's gaze. "I'm giving you my opinion, Brady. You can take it or leave it."

Joe was proud of her for standing her ground. "We're not here to talk you into anything, Elly. We sincerely wanted your opinion."

"Joe's right," Brady agreed. "You're the witness."

She took another long moment to stare at the screen, then slowly shook her head. "I'm going to say no, this is not the man I saw. But can you still dig into his background a bit? Make sure I'm not making a mistake?"

"We will," Joe assured her. "We still have enough to issue a BOLO for Colton as a person of interest." He pulled up the complaint that had been filed about Colton's actions on the job, then instantly pulled out his phone to call Assistant Chief Michaels.

"Do you have him?" Michaels asked.

Joe swallowed a sigh. Trust the assistant chief to think it's that easy. "We have a possible suspect, former cop terminated over an excessive use of force complaint. Looks like he put some guy in the hospital with a broken jaw and cracked ribs after an arrest. Oh, and his body cam wasn't working either."

"I remember that case," Michaels said. "He was an arrogant jerk, insisting he'd done nothing wrong."

"Yeah, well, difficult to prove when you put a guy in the hospital like that without video to support his side of the story," Joe drawled. "I'd like to ask one of the team members to head to his place, see if they can catch him at home."

"Go for it," Michaels agreed. "Keep me in the loop."

"Will do." He lowered the phone enough to place a call to Raelyn. Once he'd given her the information, she readily agreed. "I'll take Brock with me," she assured Joe. "We'll search high and low until we find this guy. Oh, and you should know Bartholomew Shaw's financials came back clean. We don't think he hired our shooter."

"Thanks, Rae." He lowered his phone, glad to have one name scratched from the list. Yet it bothered him to send others to do the legwork, and he found himself wondering if this was how Rhy felt when he was forced to take a leadership role in running their team.

"He put a man in the hospital?" Elly frowned. "That's awful."

"Yeah." He grimaced. "I'm wondering if this guy has a grudge against the public in general."

"Don't forget, we've only checked the Milwaukee Police Department for recent terminations," Brady added. "I have my boss putting in the same request at some of the local precincts too. Even the Brookland PD."

Elly's brown eyes widened. "I hadn't considered that possibility."

"At this point, everyone's a suspect until cleared," Joe said. He knew that most innocent people would be horrified by how cops approached a case like this. But they had twelve dead with another eight more that were wounded by this guy. As far as Joe was concerned, they didn't have a choice but to keep the suspect field wide open.

"Marc is calling again," Brady said, pulling his phone from his pocket. "Hey, Marc. Did you get more terminated cops for us to look at?"

Joe continued working on digging into Peter Colton's background while listening to Brady's side of the conversation with Marc Callahan. He paused long enough to send Steele a text message about their possible suspect.

Steele texted back with an okay sign.

"Understood. I'm on my way." Brady lowered the phone, glancing at Joe with regret. "Our boss is calling a meeting about the child abduction case. I need to go. You still have Steele watching things from across the street, right?"

"Yep." Joe nodded. "What's going on?"

"Sounds like Ian has a lead on the missing kid." Brady shrugged into his coat. "Once we get that boy reunited with his parents, we can start working on creating a three-dimensional facial recognition on our perp."

"Go." Joe didn't hesitate. He felt certain that getting the sketch through the program was their best chance of finding the guy. "We'll be okay with Steele as backup."

Brady nodded. "Good." He wrapped his arm around Elly's shoulders in a brotherly hug. "Stay safe."

"You too." After Brady left, Elly joined him at the table. "What can I do?"

He cleared his throat, trying not to be distracted by her large brown eyes. Then he turned to face her. "Maybe we should go through the shooting event one more time."

A hint of distress darkened her eyes. "If you think it will help."

He hesitated. Would it really help? Or make Elly feel worse?

"I'll do it." Elly spoke with confidence. "Where do you want me to start?"

"At the beginning." He forced himself to treat her like any other witness. He'd learned that interviewing witnesses several times often revealed new tidbits of information. Not because the witness didn't want to cooperate, but more so because once the immediate horror was past, new details emerged.

"I was looking up at the blue Christmas lights." Elly gazed off into the distance as if putting herself back there. "They were so beautiful. I remember turning to head back to the ambulance rig, and that's when I bumped into him."

He listened carefully as she recounted the brief meeting, including the way the hairs on the back of her neck lifted in alarm.

"It was dark," she admitted. "So I couldn't make out his eye color, but I have a clear image of his face imprinted on my mind." She turned to face him. "I was listening to 'Frosty the Snowman,' singing along, when I heard the gunshots and the skaters falling to the ice. From there, everything was chaos."

"I know. For me too." He hadn't been looking at the skaters or paying much attention to the marching band belting out Frosty. His gaze had been on tracking the people gathered across the street from where he was positioned.

With Kyle on the opposite side of the street doing the same thing. Yet it seemed as if the shooter had gotten several shots off before Kyle had reacted.

And that was odd, considering the shooter had likely been standing in the back of the pickup truck.

He was trying to imagine what might have drawn Kyle's attention from the shooter when his phone buzzed.

Not a text this time, but a call from Steele.

"Hey, what's up?" Joe asked.

"A black SUV has driven down the street twice in fifteen minutes." Steele's tone was terse. "You need to get Elly out of there."

"Got it." He slammed the computer shut and shoved his phone into his pocket. "Elly, grab your coat. We need to go."

"Go where?" To her credit, she didn't protest, grabbing her coat from the back of the kitchen chair and shrugging it on.

"Away from here." He reached for his own coat but didn't bother putting it on. They needed to get out of there ASAP.

The way this guy kept finding them was really starting to piss him off.

CHAPTER TWELVE

Her heart lodged in her throat, Elly stayed close behind Joe as he headed to the side door of the rental house. "Keep your head down," Joe said.

She nodded, unable to speak. It seemed impossible that they'd been found here at the rental house. It was nerve-racking to keep running from this man who was stalking her with an assault rifle, just waiting for the chance to kill her.

Joe opened the side door and peeked out. She shouldn't have been surprised to find Steele was already there, waiting for them. Rhy's tactical team worked together as if they could read each other's minds.

Maybe they could. It was painfully obvious that she would never have made it as a cop. Even if she could have passed the physical.

"This way," Steele said in a low hushed tone.

Joe urged her forward, placing her between the two men. She hated the necessity of Joe and Steele putting their lives on the line for her. They moved along the back of the house, out of sight of the road. She didn't know what Steele had seen, but she trusted him to lead them to safety.

The silence was only broken by the sounds of their footsteps crunching in the snow. She tried to step carefully and quietly but couldn't. How Steele and Joe were able to master the art of moving without making a sound, she had no idea.

Steele paused at the corner of the house, then whispered, "Stay close."

She nodded.

Steele picked up the pace, cutting across the yard, heading from their rental house to the next property. She could feel Joe's reassuring hand on her back as she followed Steele.

It was midmorning, with an overcast sky overhead. There were no lights on in the house they were hiding behind, but that didn't mean there weren't people inside. What if one of them noticed them trespassing and called the police?

Better the police than the shooter.

"Down!" Steele's harsh whisper caught her off guard. She dropped into a crouch, plastering herself against the brick exterior of the house.

Joe moved forward so that he was practically curled around her. For long moments, no one moved as they strained to listen.

Elly couldn't hear anything beyond her own heartbeat. Then Steele slowly rose to his feet. She and Joe followed suit.

"Where did you stash the SUV?" Joe asked.

"It's on the other side of the road," Steele said in a hushed voice. "We'll need to cross at some point. Probably one more house down."

"Got it," Joe agreed.

"Let's go." Steele once again moved along the back of

the neighbor's house. Thankfully, if there was someone inside, they didn't raise an alarm.

When Steele reached the corner, he once again paused to look toward the road. Apparently seeing nothing alarming, he crossed the open area between the properties to reach the next house.

She inwardly braced for someone to throw open a door or window asking what they were doing. But maybe because homes were closed up tight in the winter, no one seemed to notice them.

At the corner of the third house, Steele glanced at Joe. "Ready?"

"Yes." Joe's expression was tense, but he didn't look alarmed. "Let's do it."

Steele waited another moment, his head swiveling from side to side before he turned the corner and broke into a jog.

Elly did the same, giving up any attempt to move stealthily. Joe stayed so close behind her she could hear him breathing. When they made it across the road, Steele headed straight through that neighbor's yard.

She felt certain their luck wouldn't hold forever. One of these residents would notice them and either call the police or say something. Steele acted as if this was something they did on a regular basis.

When Steele reached the backyard, she fully expected him to follow the back of the house to the next property again. But he didn't. He went straight through yet another backyard to reach the next block.

There, he turned right. When he abruptly stopped near an SUV, she almost plowed into him. Joe caught the back of her jacket, holding her steady.

Steele lifted the key fob to unlock the doors. Then he

opened the rear passenger door. "Go ahead and climb in," he whispered.

She didn't need any prodding. After scrambling inside, she gratefully latched her seat belt. Steele shut her door, then ran around to the driver's side. Joe slid into the seat in front of her.

Steele started the engine, then pulled slowly away from the curb. She'd expected him to speed away, but he didn't.

"Elly, bend over so you're not visible," Joe said.

She had to remove the shoulder strap to accomplish that feat. Bending at the waist, she rested her forehead on her knees.

"Did you get a license plate of the vehicle that cruised past the safe house?" Joe asked.

"No, because the front plate was missing, and the rear plate was covered with mud," Steele replied. "That's what raised my suspicions in the first place. After he drove by a second time, I knew we needed to get Elly out of there."

"Thanks for sounding the alarm." Joe still sounded tense. "But I'd really like to know how we were found."

"I would too," Steele said. "Stay alert. This guy is known for shooting at targets from a higher ground."

That made her sit up. "What if he takes out the two of you?"

"Get back down, Elly." Joe's tone was firm. "You're the target here, not us."

She lowered her forehead back to her knees. "This guy has already killed twelve people. You really think he'll balk at taking out two more to get to me?"

There was a long silence, before Joe said, "Don't worry. We won't let that happen."

They would *try* not to let that happen. But Elly knew

anything was possible. Especially since they were dealing with a man with no heart and no soul.

But she kept her thoughts to herself. Because she had no choice but to trust in Joe and Steele's skills.

And of course, she had faith in God's strength and wisdom.

That thought helped ease her anxiety. She wasn't in control, God was. She would trust in Him and His plan for them.

Whatever that plan might be.

"Turn!" Joe's shout came a split second before Steele cranked the wheel. Unprepared, she lurched sideways, her head bouncing against the door.

A sharp crack of gunfire rang out, followed by a muffled thunk as the bullet struck the vehicle.

"Go!" Joe shouted. Not that he needed to as Steele hit the gas, sending the SUV speeding forward.

It wasn't easy to keep her head down, unable to anticipate his next move. She reached out and grabbed the door handle, trying to keep herself from flopping from one side to the other like a dead fish.

Then she caught the strong scent of gasoline.

"Tank is hit; we're losing fuel," Steele said in a clipped tone. "Call Brady or one of the other Finnegans. We need back up ASAP."

"Brady, where are you?" Joe's voice was calm. "We've been hit by gunfire and need backup."

There was a long silence as Joe listened. The car continued to make one sharp turn after another until she feared she'd be sick.

Then Joe said, "Good. We'll head there, thanks."

She wasn't worried, she knew Brady or one of her other brothers would come for them.

The only question was when. And if her siblings would get there before the gunman tracked them down.

JOE WAS HANGING onto his temper with an effort. Getting angry was useless. They'd figure out later how they'd been found. Their only priority was to get Elly to safety.

Before running out of gas.

"Do you know where Rosie's Diner is?" Joe asked Steele.

"Yeah." Steele's expression was grim. "Not sure we'll make it that far."

"We can walk the last mile or so if needed." Joe had been doing his best to be on alert for another threat. Thankfully, he'd glimpsed the shadow up in the tree in time to avoid a direct hit.

But still not soon enough to avoid their vehicle being damaged.

Without warning, the vehicle began to slow. Steele thumped the steering wheel with the palm of his hand in frustration. "Come on, come on," he muttered.

"Turn left." Joe had noticed a sign indicating there was no through traffic. A dead-end street was probably the best place to leave the car. "We'll walk from here."

Steele cranked the wheel. The vehicle rolled slowly, then came to a stop. "This is the end of the train."

"That's fine. Rosie's is only a mile away." Joe pushed out of the car door, then opened the rear door to let Elly out. "Maybe less if we take shortcuts."

"Fine with me," Steele agreed.

"That's a little risky, isn't it?" Elly asked. Joe noticed her fingers were shaking as she tucked a strand of hair behind her ear. "Someone might call the cops."

"No matter. We are the cops." Joe managed a reassuring smile. "Can you make it a little farther?"

"Of course." Despite her pale face and trembling fingers, she looked determined. "I've heard about Rosie's, apparently it's Colin's favorite place to eat breakfast, but have never been there."

He was glad she was holding it together. At least for now. He didn't doubt that reaction would set in at some point.

And he silently vowed to be there for her when it did.

"We're going to use the same formation," he told Elly. "You follow Steele; I'll cover your back."

"Okay." He was glad she didn't argue.

Steele scanned the area, then chose a path. Elly didn't hesitate to follow. Joe stayed close to Elly, trusting his teammate to get them to Rosie's.

It was a good thing dark clouds hovered low on the horizon. He'd take whatever bit of camouflage he could get.

They moved through one backyard after another. At one point, Elly stumbled. He grabbed onto the back of her coat, hauling her back upright. She tossed him a grateful look over her shoulder. He almost told Steele to slow down but decided against it. They couldn't afford to linger. Being on the move was the best way to stay ahead of this guy.

How on earth had they been found at four separate and distinctly different safe house locations?

He didn't have to wonder what Rhy would say about this. He already knew. They had to have been followed or tracked somehow.

And they needed to figure out how before they moved on.

After ten minutes, Steele slowed, glancing back at him. Steele gestured toward the gas station, and he nodded in agreement.

Once they were safely behind the building, Steele asked, "Rosie's is another seven to eight blocks from here. Do you want to keep pushing forward? Or see if Brady can come here to pick us up?"

"Quinn and Sami are the ones meeting us at the restaurant," Joe said. "Brady and Marc are still tied up at the bureau."

Steele nodded. "I know Sami. She's a great cop."

"Yes, she is," Elly said.

He glanced at his watch. "I agree, but I don't think they're at the restaurant yet. Let's keep going."

Elly had been leaning against the building, looking out of breath. When she realized Joe and Steele were looking at her, she straightened and lifted her chin. "I can go another seven blocks, no problem."

He wanted to haul her into his arms for a kiss. He admired her spunk in the face of adversity. In the face of a seemingly never-ending threat.

Elly may be the baby of the Finnegan family, but she had the same grit and determination as the rest of them.

"Ready?" Steele's question pulled him from his thoughts.

"Lead the way." He rested his hand on the small of Elly's back, gently urging her forward.

They didn't have to cut through people's yards anymore, as there were businesses lining each side of the street. He watched the traffic closely as they headed down the sidewalk.

Steele did take a few extra turns, taking them out of

their way. If Elly was upset about the extra walking, she didn't let on.

Finally, Steele crossed the street to Rosie's. The diner wasn't large, but Joe noticed there were several people sitting at booths inside. People going about their lives as usual as if there wasn't a crazed shooter on the loose. Steele held the door for them. Joe followed Elly inside, grateful for the warmth that enveloped them.

"Ach, who have we here?" A distinct Irish brogue had him glancing toward a round woman carrying a tray of what looked like fresh apple turnovers. "Another Finnegan, ain't ya?"

"Me?" Elly looked confused. "Um, yes."

"Aye, lass, you look like Colin and Aiden, don't ya?" The woman beamed. "Let's get you a table."

Joe stepped forward. "You must be Rosie. We have Quinn and Sami joining us."

"Brilliant!" Rosie took them to a round table with five place settings. Then she whirled away to deliver the apple turnovers to another table.

"I want what they're having." Steele followed Rosie with his gaze. "Smells delicious."

"I can't believe she recognized me." Elly looked bemused as she dropped into the seat between him and Steele.

"The Finnegans share a lot of family traits," Joe pointed out.

Rosie returned with coffee and mugs. Before she could say anything, Steele said, "I'd love one of your apple turnovers."

"Ach, yes, of course ya will, lad! I'll bring them straight over." Rosie bustled away.

"I haven't been a lad for a long time, but I'm not

complaining," Steele joked. "That woman can call me anything she likes."

Joe leaned forward. "We need to understand how we were tracked to the rental."

All hint of humor faded from Steele's gaze. "I know. That was too close for comfort."

Rosie returned with a tray full of pastries. Despite their having eaten breakfast earlier, Joe offered the tray to Elly, then took one for himself before passing it down to Steele.

"You mentioned this guy is either a cop or military, right?" Elly took a small bite of the apple turnover. "Hmm. Very good."

Joe had to admit Rosie could bake. "Yes, but if he was terminated, how is he getting his intel? That's the part that doesn't make sense."

"We got rid of our phones." Elly frowned. "But what about you, Steele? Could he have tracked you somehow?"

"Maybe." Steele took another bite of his turnover before answering. "But how would he know I'm even involved?"

Joe's stomach knotted. "Maybe because he's been watching us longer than we know. Or he recognized you."

"Or he knows Rhy and the members of the tactical team," Elly added. "You may have been mentioned during one of the many times the sibs have been in danger."

There was a long silence as Joe and Steele exchanged grim looks. "Okay, we can get rid of Steele's phone," he said. "But there must be other precautions we can take."

"A motel that takes only cash is our only option," Steele said. "We can't leave any sort of paper trail."

"I need to get in touch with Tarin. He had access to a safe house a while back that would be perfect for Elly." He popped the last bit of apple turnover into his mouth, then took a sip of coffee. "I'll get his number from Quinn."

"I know it," Elly said. He glanced at her in surprise when she rattled it off.

He punched the digits into his phone. Tarin didn't pick up, so he left a message about Elly needing a safe house along with his number.

"There you are," Quinn said.

He pushed the phone back into his pocket and turned to find Quinn and Sami making their way through the crowded diner.

"Hi, Quinn. Sami." Elly stood and enveloped her brother and sister-in-law in a hug. "It's nice to see you."

Quinn scowled at the empty plate of turnovers. "You chowhounds ate them all?"

"Rosie will bring more." Steele grinned. "I hear you Finnegans stab each other with forks to fight over food."

"That was Colin and Aiden." Quinn narrowed his gaze. "But don't push me, Delaney. I'll stab you if you touch my turnover."

"Can we please get back to the issue of keeping Elly safe?" Joe was irritated with the banter. "Quinn, I left Tarin a message about using the safe house. We've been found four times in two days."

"That's not good," Sami said. "How are you being tracked?"

"I'm not sure." And that was the most frustrating part of all. "We think he's a cop and maybe knows the tactical team is involved in keeping Elly safe."

"That's not a stretch," Sami agreed. "The Finnegans are well known in the area. And the cop grapevine is always alive and active."

Joe should have forced the issue of the entire team using disposable phones. But he'd honestly thought they'd have this guy in custody by now. It was highly unusual for a high-profile killer to evade law enforcement like this.

"Ach, there's Quinn and Sami!" Rosie set another plate of turnovers on the table. "Would ya all be having breakfast, too, then?"

"Not me," Elly said. "The apple turnover was more than enough."

"I'm good too," Joe said. "But the others probably need to eat."

It only took a minute for Steele, Quinn, and Sami to place their breakfast orders. When they were alone again, Joe leaned forward. "We really need to find this guy. Any ideas?"

Sami grimaced. "Every squad on the street has the sketch and is searching for him. The stolen truck didn't give us any viable leads either."

"What about that one guy, Peter Colton?" Steele asked. "He's a terminated cop with a face that's a pseudo match for the sketch."

"A pseudo match?" Sami asked.

Elly frowned. "His picture doesn't match the sketch as well as I would have liked. It also doesn't match the memory fragment in my mind. Although my encounter with him was brief, so it's possible Colton is our guy."

"Raelyn and Brock were supposed to go to his last known residence to find him," Joe added. "But we haven't heard anything since."

"That's good to hear," Sami said. "I'd think you would be the first to know once they have him in custody."

Joe wasn't as convinced as she was about Assistant Chief Michaels's intent to keep him in the loop. His boss had demanded Joe keep the assistant chief informed on what was happening, but that didn't mean communication would flow both ways. "Maybe. I'll check in later."

"This place is nice," Elly said, glancing around. "I can see why Colin likes it."

"Colin likes to eat, period," Quinn said with a grin. "You ask me, he's a frustrated chef working as a firefighter."

Joe nursed his coffee, wishing Tarin would get back to him about the safe house. Granted, the guy was probably working, but still, his sister's life was on the line.

A few minutes later, Rosie returned with a large tray laden with plates of food. Joe shook his head at the heaping portions placed in front of Quinn and Steele. Sami's was a normal-sized breakfast.

"You guys are acting like you haven't eaten in months." He gave them an exasperated look. "And here I thought you'd chosen this place because it was best for Elly."

"It is," Quinn insisted. Then he scowled. "Why aren't you two eating?"

"I already cooked breakfast for me and Joe," Elly said. "Hurry up and eat. We're waiting on you to get out of here."

Quinn sent him a level stare at the cooking breakfast comment, which Joe immediately interpreted as a warning not to cross the line with Elly. He wondered if Brady had already told the rest of the siblings about his kissing their sister.

Then he dismissed the idea. For one thing, he would have heard directly from Rhy himself if that was the case. And besides, there hadn't been enough time for the rumor mill to have churned through that information.

But it would get through to the rest of the family at some point. It was only a matter of time.

Quinn said grace, then dove into his meal. Sami caught his gaze. "What happened to the SUV?"

Joe quickly filled them in on the SUV that Steele had noticed driving past the rental property twice in ten minutes, minus a front license plate and a covered rear plate. Then the shadow in the tree, followed by gunfire.

"Dude managed to plant a bullet in the fuel tank, so we abandoned it and covered the rest of the ground on foot," Steele said. "Elly has been great through all of this."

The compliment had Joe grinding his molars together. Not that Steele had so much as flirted with Elly, but still. He didn't like it.

"I hate being this guy's target." Elly frowned. "I'll feel awful if anything happens to any of you."

"It's our job to keep you safe," Joe said as his phone buzzed. He glanced at the screen, expecting to see Tarin's number, but it was Brock. He lifted the phone to his ear, plugging his other ear to hear better. "What's going on?"

"We have Peter Colton in custody." Brock got straight to the point. "We'd been watching his place, and he just showed up, making it a little too easy for us. Even better, we found a rifle and a handgun in his residence. No assault weapon, though, so he probably ditched it."

Joe glanced at his watch. It was an hour since the gunman had fired on their SUV. Was that enough time for Colton to get back to his place? "I'm glad you have him, along with the rifle and handgun, but what's Colton's address?"

Brock rattled it off. Joe envisioned the area. Less than fifteen minutes from Rosie's dinner, which made it entirely possible they had their shooter.

"Who's going to interview him?" Joe asked.

"We thought you'd want to be involved," Brock said. "Otherwise, Rae and I can do it."

"I want to be there." He caught Sami's gaze. The

hopeful glint in her eye indicated she understood what was going on. "Give us twenty minutes, okay?"

"Sure thing." Brock disconnected from the call.

Joe hoped Sami and Quinn brought a spare vehicle for them to use. Despite the way he'd wanted to keep Elly sheltered in a safe place, that hadn't been working too well. Maybe the danger was over, but he wasn't letting Elly out of his sight.

Not until he knew without a shadow of doubt that they had the Christmas parade shooter safely behind bars.

CHAPTER THIRTEEN

Having Peter Colton in custody was a relief. Even though Elly hadn't been convinced he was the shooter, the fact that Brock and Raelyn had found a rifle and a handgun was encouraging. Not illegal, though, unless one of the weapons had been used while committing a crime.

She desperately wanted this nightmare to be over. Yes, she would miss spending time with Joe, but the longer this evil man was out there stalking her, the more likely innocent victims would be hurt.

Or killed.

"We need to get over to the precinct to interview Peter Colton," Joe said. "We also need a vehicle."

"You can use ours," Quinn quickly offered. "We can call one of the sibs for a ride home."

"Thanks, Quinn." Elly knew her family would come through for them. "We appreciate your support."

"Have you spoken to Rhy lately?" Quinn asked.

She winced. "No, but we will."

Her brother held her gaze. "Do that soon, El. You know he worries about you."

It wasn't easy being the youngest of nine. She loved her family, but they tended to hover. And maybe that was partially her own fault, she silently admitted. After all, she could have moved out of the homestead. She'd actually made plans to do that but then decided to stay longer to help Devon with the baby.

"I promise to call Rhy." She managed a smile. "I'm sure it's frustrating for him to be left out of the action."

"Big time, not that he would willingly leave Devon and Colleen behind," Quinn agreed.

Sensing Joe's impatience, she glanced at him. His grim expression made her wish she could lighten his burden. None of this was his fault. Maybe if she hadn't bumped into the shooter, making eye contact with him, they wouldn't be in danger now.

But she couldn't go back and change the past no matter how much she wanted to.

"I'm almost finished." Steele looked pointedly at Joe's tapping fingers. "I'll ride with you back to the precinct."

"Thanks." Joe looked relieved.

True to his word, Steele finished his breakfast in record time. Joe pulled cash from his pocket, but Quinn waved it off.

"I'll take care of it," her brother assured him. "We have to hang around for a while until one of the sibs can pick us up."

"Or use a rideshare," Steele suggested.

"That too," Quinn agreed. He tossed Joe the key fob, then added, "Keep Elly safe."

"That's the plan." Joe stood and held her coat for her. She slipped her arms into the winter jacket, feeling self-conscious as Quinn watched.

"Thanks," she murmured, zipping it up over the vest.

Joe and Steele donned their jackets too, then made their way through Rosie's Diner. The place was hopping, so they didn't have a chance to tell Rosie goodbye.

Outside, Joe clicked the key fob to find Quinn's SUV. Soon they were buckled in and heading toward the precinct. Elly folded her hands in her lap, feeling nervous about seeing the Christmas parade shooter in person.

As if sensing her distress, Joe caught her glance in the rearview mirror. "We'll make sure you're behind the two-way mirror so he can't see you."

"I understand." She put on a brave front.

"Too bad we can't do a lineup," Steele muttered.

"I know, that's my fault for showing Elly Colton's photo," Joe agreed. "But we'll get him. He may spill something during the interview."

And if he didn't? Elly didn't voice the thought.

Joe escorted her to an interview room. Through the one-way glass, she got her first glimpse of Peter Colton in the flesh. The minute she saw him, she knew he wasn't the shooter.

She didn't have a photographic memory or anything like that. But the image of the gunman was indelibly etched in her mind. There wasn't time to say anything to Joe or Steele though as they entered the room, joining Brock and Colton.

They introduced themselves, then sat across from the former cop.

"Do you want a lawyer?" Joe asked.

Colton crossed his arms over his chest. "I don't need one. I didn't shoot anyone. You don't have anything on me other than some vague similarity to a sketch. I'm not your guy."

She continued to listen as Joe, Brock, and Steele questioned Colton.

"Were you at the Christmas parade?" Joe asked.

"No, I was home. Alone," Colton added. "I had no reason to go to a stupid parade. I don't even like Christmas."

"Why were you fired from the police department?" Brock asked.

Colton scowled. "I'm sure you know that already. A lowlife scumbag claimed I used excessive force during his arrest."

"Did you?" Joe asked.

Colton narrowed his gaze. "I don't have to answer that."

There was a long moment of silence as the four men stared at each other.

Finally, Joe slid the photos of the dead skaters across the table. "Do you know these victims?" Elly caught a glimpse of surprise and shock in Colton's eyes. As if he couldn't believe how brutally they'd been murdered.

"No. Why would I?" Colton shoved the photos back. "I already told you I wasn't at the stupid parade."

"You've never seen them?" Joe pressed.

Colton shrugged. "I may have seen the ice skaters on TV. They're in a commercial I think, aren't they?" When Joe didn't respond, he added, "Seeing them isn't knowing them. I've never met either of them in person."

"Do you own any guns?" Steele asked.

Colton snorted. "You found the rifle and handgun. They're both legal and registered. You have my concealed carry permit. No, I don't have any other guns."

The guys asked several more questions before Colton himself ended the interview.

"Enough." He scowled. "I've cooperated with these ridiculous allegations. You can either arrest me or let me go."

"You're not finished until we say so," Brock challenged.

"In that case, I'll call my lawyer." Colton wasn't fazed

by the threat. "He'll have me out of here in five minutes flat. You don't have anything linking me to this crime because I wasn't there. I didn't do this."

Elly could tell that the guys were frustrated by the lack of information they were getting from the interview. But since Colton asked for his lawyer, there wasn't anything more they could do.

"You're free to go," Joe said. "For now."

Colton shot him a narrow glare but didn't respond. Elly watched as the four men filed out of the interview room.

"This way," Brock said, escorting Colton away.

Joe and Steele came around to meet with her. "What did you think?" Joe asked.

"He's not the shooter." She hadn't meant to come across so bluntly.

"How can you be sure?" Joe clearly didn't want to let it go.

A flash of annoyance hit hard. "I told you before, when I first saw his photograph, that he didn't look like the shooter. Even if he'd done something to change his features, he doesn't match my memory. Especially his eyes. I know I'll recognize them when I see him." She lifted her chin, meeting Joe's gaze head-on. "I'm telling you, that is not the man I bumped into at the Christmas parade."

"You admitted to seeing him for less than a minute," Joe said stubbornly. "You could be mistaken."

"I'm not." She stepped closer, stabbing her index finger into Joe's chest. "He's not the shooter."

"Hold on, Elly," Steele said. "We believe you."

"Joe doesn't." She didn't take her gaze off his. "I understand you want this nightmare over. Don't you think I feel the same way? I prayed we'd found him. But Peter Colton isn't the shooter." She jabbed his chest again for emphasis.

She tried to dial back her anger, but it wasn't easy. Arresting the wrong guy wouldn't make her feel safe.

That would only happen when they found and arrested the real culprit

JOE LIFTED his hands in surrender. "Okay, okay. I hear you."

"It's about time." Elly stepped back, dragging her hand through her hair. He'd never seen her so annoyed and angry. And really, he couldn't help but be impressed by how she'd stood up to him.

She might be Rhy's baby sister, but she wasn't a wimp. She stood up for what she believed. And of course, she'd saved his life that night, handling the shooting scene like a professional.

He was forced to admit that if Elly said Colton wasn't their guy, he needed to believe her. His glimpse of the shooter had been from a distance. She'd seen him up close.

"I trust you, Elly," he finally said. "You would recognize the shooter more than I would."

"Thank you." Her voice didn't necessarily reflect gratitude.

"We don't have anything on Colton anyway," Steele said, his gaze darting between him and Elly as if watching a ping-pong match. "The lab will compare the shell casings from Colton's weapon to those found at the crime scene. I doubt they'll match."

"They won't because the shooter had an AK-47." Joe knew Steele was right. Besides, Colton hadn't given them anything useful. The guy didn't have an alibi, but that didn't make him a stone-cold killer.

Yet he hated knowing that without Colton, they were back at square one.

"Now what?" Elly asked.

He sighed. "I need to update Michaels. You should call Rhy to fill him in on the latest. He should know that Colton isn't our guy."

"Okay." Elly pulled out her disposable cell to make the call.

"I'll watch her," Steele said in a low tone. "Go chat with Michaels."

He nodded and turned away. He found Michaels in his office. The guy waved him in.

"Did Colton give you anything?" Assistant Chief Michaels asked.

"No. Ms. Elly Finnegan doesn't believe he's our guy." He briefly summarized the disappointing results of the interview.

"How reliable is your witness?" Michaels asked.

"Very." He didn't hesitate. "She bumped into him, saw him up close. I'm convinced she would know him if she saw him again."

"That's just great," Michaels muttered. "We've got a whole lot of nothing."

"I know. But I still believe the shooter's background is either as a cop or being in the military." He went on to explain the way their most recent safe house had been found. "We're barely managing to stay one step ahead of this guy."

"We need another lead." Michaels rubbed his hand over his chin. "Got any ideas?"

He desperately wished he did. "We'll keep going through the witness list. This guy opened fire on the paradegoers for a reason."

"Yeah." Michaels sat back in his chair. "I appreciate the update, Kingsley. But there is one more thing you should know."

"Like what?" Had he missed some other avenue to investigate this case?

"Captain Finnegan put in a request for you to be promoted to lieutenant. It took a while for the upper brass to approve your promotion and rank, but it's official. Or will be at the first of the year."

"Lieutenant?" Joe tried to hide his shock. He knew Rhy often leaned on him as the team leader, but to recommend him for a promotion? That was a surprise. "Thank you, sir."

"You earned it." Michaels waved away his gratitude. "Keep up the good work."

He'd done a far from stellar job on this case, but he simply nodded. "Will do. Thanks again." He turned and left the office.

The bump in pay would be good, especially if Elly didn't want to keep working as an EMT. As soon as the thought entered his mind, he mentally kicked himself. What was he thinking? He didn't have a claim on Elly. No matter how much he liked and admired her.

And even though he wanted nothing more than to see her again once this was over, he had Rhy and the rest of the Finnegan siblings to deal with. He imagined Rhy would regret submitting his name for a promotion if he knew how Joe had kissed Elly.

And how badly he wanted to kiss her again.

Enough. He couldn't think about a potential future with Elly. Not until they had the shooter behind bars.

As he rounded the corner, he saw Grayson chatting with Elly. Steele wasn't around, and he found himself curling his fingers into fists when he caught sight of Elly laughing at something Grayson was saying.

The stab of adolescent jealousy hit hard. Grayson was known to be a chick magnet. For whatever reason, women gravitated toward him. It was all he could do not to physically insert himself between Grayson and Elly.

"Hey, where's Steele?" Joe asked in what he hoped was a nonchalant voice as he approached.

Elly turned to face him, her eyes brightening when she saw him. "I'm glad you're back, Joe. Steele is arranging for another vehicle for us to use."

"Great." He forced himself to relax. Elly had looked pleased to see him. Maybe he wouldn't have to punch Grayson in the nose.

Grayson's dark eyes shifted between him and Elly as understanding dawned. Joe held his teammate's gaze, refusing to back down. He knew he was treading on thin ice but couldn't find the energy to care. He was way past trying to keep himself from becoming emotionally involved. That ship had obviously sailed. He decided it would be best for the entire tactical team to know he had personal feelings for Elly.

They'd need every minute of their intense skill and training to keep her safe.

"There he is now." Grayson nodded toward the doorway. Steele crossed the room, holding up a set of keys.

"I've secured you a new ride," he announced. "Figured I could return Quinn and Sami's SUV. Grayson can follow along to give me a ride back."

"Are they still at Rosie's?" Elly asked.

"Yep." Steele dropped the key fob into Joe's outstretched hand. "We can meet up with you at the safe house."

Joe frowned. "What safe house?"

"Oh, that's right. I forgot to tell you. Tarin came through for us," Elly said. "I talked to him after touching base with Rhy. We're all set."

"That's great news." He was glad to have a plan. "Okay, we'll head over there now. I want the two of you to escort us to the replacement vehicle, though, considering the last time we drew gunfire."

"Got it," Steele agreed.

"Count me in too," Grayson added.

"Steele, you and Grayson can meet up with us, but only after you get replacement phones." He scowled. "We're not taking any more chances with this guy finding us at the safe house."

"Understood." Steele clapped Grayson on the back. "Let's hit the road."

"Do I get to eat breakfast too?" Grayson asked as they made their way to the side exit. "I'm hungry. I heard all about Rosie's apple turnovers."

Joe ignored their banter. He held Elly back until Steele and Grayson had stepped outside. Then he urged Elly across the threshold, keeping her sandwiched between the three men. They moved as a group to the SUV parked close to the building.

There was no gunfire this time, giving Joe hope that they'd gotten away clean. Although he wouldn't relax until he had Elly stashed inside the safe house, behind bullet-resistant glass windows.

"Why didn't Tarin call me?" He glanced at Elly. "I'm the one who left him a message."

"He was going to, but I got to him first." She shrugged. "He would have called sooner but had to wait until the family had been relocated and the cleaning crew had come in."

"He arranged that just for you?" Joe was surprised Tarin had the support of the department to pull rank like that. Granted, Rhy was a captain, and the department tended to take care of their own.

"No, they were scheduled to go to a new location in another state anyway." Elly frowned. "I hope they're okay. I hate the idea of children being in danger. They deserve the safe house more than I do."

"I'm sure they're fine." He couldn't worry about the family Tarin had relocated, not when there was a vicious gunman stalking Elly for the past two days. "They wouldn't have been moved if it wasn't safe to do so."

"I hope not." Elly settled back in her seat as he drove away from the precinct. "I have to wonder if the real shooter knew you had Peter Colton in custody. He could assume the pressure is off."

He glanced at her in admiration. "That's possible. He could have a scanner. Maybe that's why he didn't bother staking out the police department again. Well, that and we had already canvassed the area after the last attempt. Not very smart to push his luck by taking that same shot a second time in two days."

"Yeah, maybe." She looked thoughtful. "Did Assistant Chief Michaels have any insights to share?"

"Not really." He shrugged. "Your brother put my name in for a promotion to lieutenant. The upper brass approved the new rank and pay increase, effective the first week of January."

"Really?" Elly turned in his seat to take his arm. "Oh, Joe, that's wonderful! I'm so happy for you."

"Thanks." He could feel his face heating up. "It's nice of your brother to do that. I hope to make him proud."

"Rhy has always leaned on your leadership, Joe. He wouldn't recommend you if he didn't trust and believe in you."

Yeah, that was what he was afraid of. That Rhy's trust and admiration would fade like the mist once he made it clear he wanted to ask Elly out.

They couldn't demote him for that, could they?

Nah, he didn't think so. That wasn't how the upper echelon within the police department worked. Although Rhy could make his life extremely difficult if he wanted to. Would Elly's brother stoop that low?

He hoped not.

Yet there was no point in thinking about that now. Elly's safety trumped everything else. He'd gladly give up his promotion if he thought that would help find and arrest the shooter.

"Joe? I think the safe house is in the other direction."

"Yes, I know." He smiled reassuringly. "It's become a habit to take the long route to our destination."

"I understand." She sighed. "I wish there was more we could do to find this guy. I hate knowing he's planning to strike out at me again."

That was a massive understatement. "Me too. But keep your faith, Elly. You've said from the beginning that God has a plan for us. We'll find him."

"I know we will." Her smile was strained.

His phone rang. He pulled it from his pocket, surprised to see the call had the first three numbers of the police station. "Kingsley."

"This is Josie from dispatch. I just got a call from Eloise

Malaki." It took him a moment to place the name of Kyle's widow. "She thinks there's a man outside her house."

A shiver snaked down his spine. "Patch me through to her."

"Will do." The dispatcher spoke to Eloise, then dropped off the call.

"Is this Joe?" Eloise's voice was barely above a whisper.

"Yes. Do you recognize the man outside your house? What does he look like?" Joe asked.

"He's wearing a long coat, but he's too far away for me to see him clearly." Eloise's whisper was full of fear. "Please, Joe. I don't want to die."

"Go into the bathroom and lock the door. Take a weapon with you if you have one." He wanted to assure her that everything would be fine, but he couldn't. "We'll be there as soon as possible, okay?"

"Hurry." She abruptly disconnected from the line.

"What's going on?" Elly gripped the armrest as he hit the gas, taking a sharp right toward Greenland where he knew Kyle and Eloise lived.

"Eloise saw a man outside her house." He thrust the phone into her hand. "Call dispatch back, tell them we need all units to respond to her address." He gave her the house number and street information.

Elly did as he'd asked, speaking in a calm tone despite the seriousness of the situation. When that call was finished, she went ahead and called Steele and Grayson too.

"The shooter was last seen at Kyle and Eloise's house," she said. "We're heading there now. Joe needs backup."

He concentrated on driving, desperately wishing he could drop Elly someplace safe. Taking her on a call like this wasn't smart. But he couldn't bear the thought of letting this guy slip away either.

And why would the shooter show up at Eloise's home anyway? Because Kyle had been the true target all along? They'd felt certain the two ice skaters had been killed first. But maybe that had been done to clear the area for a better angle to eliminate Kyle.

It was a possibility that hadn't occurred to him until now.

"Steele and Grayson are meeting us there," Elly said. "What did Eloise say?"

"She saw a man in a long coat." Even as he said the words, he frowned. "Seems odd that he'd still have that long coat on. Too noticeable."

"Rhy claims criminals aren't always smart." Her voice wavered a bit, betraying her fear.

"He's right about that." He pressed harder on the accelerator, taking the shortest route to Eloise's home.

While praying with all his heart that they wouldn't get there too late.

CHAPTER FOURTEEN

Elly's heart thundered in her chest as Joe navigated the suburban neighborhood that wasn't far from the precinct. She wanted to believe they would find and arrest the shooter, but despite Rhy's wise words, she couldn't imagine this guy would allow himself to be caught so easily.

He'd avoided detection so far, hadn't he?

The houses in this area were closer together than where they lived in Brookland. She frowned, wondering if the shooter lived in the neighborhood too. The same way Eloise and Kyle had.

But if that was the case, why hadn't anyone turned him in to the authorities? Neighbors would obviously know each other. Or at least see them coming and going on occasion. It was inconceivable that anyone would secretly harbor a cold-blooded killer.

"You're still wearing your vest?" Joe glanced at her as if to see for himself.

"Yes." She was glad that Joe and the other guys were equally outfitted. Not that a vest would save them from a shooter aiming for their heads. She swallowed hard and pressed a hand to her stomach.

Rhy had once mentioned that head shots were difficult to make because the target was so small. And that cops were trained to aim for center mass, chest and abdomen. She hoped and prayed this shooter would do the same.

She couldn't bear the thought of anything happening to Joe. Or anyone else on the tactical team.

Joe pulled over to the side of the road. "Her house is the brown ranch second in on the left side of the street. Keep your head down, Elly."

"Okay." She ducked in her seat, hugging her knees. "I didn't see anyone, though, did you?"

"Not yet." His tone was tense, and she belatedly realized her talking was a distraction. Something he and the rest of the team could ill afford. She tried to hold back from asking any more questions, although it wasn't easy. She was naturally a chatty person.

The possibility of this being a trap gnawed at her. Hard to imagine that Eloise would have done such a thing, but obviously some people had no moral code.

Like the shooter himself.

A shiver skimmed down her spine. She didn't like this one little bit.

"Grayson and Steele are here," Joe said for her benefit. "They're going to canvass the area."

"By themselves?" She turned her head to look up at him. "They should wait for more backup."

"Raelyn and Brock are en route." His expression could have been carved from stone. "I'm sure other officers will arrive on scene soon too."

She was glad more team members were on their way. "What about Eloise? What if the shooter is inside?"

"Good point. I'll check." Joe made the call, a few seconds passing before he said, "Eloise, are you okay?"

She strained to hear the response but couldn't. Likely the frightened woman was hiding in the bathroom as Joe had instructed her to do.

"Okay, sit tight. We don't see anyone out here yet, but I have the team encircling the area." Another pause, then he added, "We'll let you know."

"She's okay, then?" Elly asked as he put his phone away.

"Yeah." Joe sighed. "It looks like the immediate area is clear. Maybe he took off, or maybe she saw someone else. I'd really like to go inside to talk to Eloise in more detail."

"You should." She understood he was holding back because of her. "I'll be fine."

Joe held her gaze for a long moment. He opened his mouth as if to say something, but then turned away and slid out from behind the wheel. "Grayson? I want you to stand guard over Elly. Raelyn and Brock, I want you stationed on either side of the property. Steele, you cover the back. I'm going in to speak to Eloise."

"You shouldn't go in alone," Steele said. "I've cleared the back. Let me come with you."

Elly held her breath, praying Joe would go along with that plan. She didn't know why she had a bad feeling about this.

"Fine." Joe's tone was clipped. "But I want Raelyn and Brock to keep an eye on the rear side of the house too. Maybe position yourselves catty-corner so you can watch both the back and the front."

"Done," Brock agreed.

"Let's go." Joe slammed the car door shut. Elly lifted her head just enough to watch Joe and Steele approach the brown ranch to speak with Kyle's widow. She thought about how Kyle had tried to talk to her before he'd died. He'd called her name.

Or maybe he'd mistaken her for his wife, Eloise.

She replayed those frantic moments in her mind. Kyle had recognized her, calling her Elly. He'd been to the homestead often enough.

She'd assumed Kyle had wanted to give her a message for his wife, Eloise. But what if he'd been trying to warn her? Mere seconds before he'd lapsed unconscious and died in the street.

She told herself not to think about all the blood oozing from Kyle's body. She needed to stay focused on what had happened that night.

It didn't seem likely that the shooter would come to the parade simply to kill Kyle while he was on duty. Why not take the cop out when he was working on the yard or running errands? As it was, the bullet had struck Kyle in the upper thigh, right beneath the location of the vest, which is why he'd bled out. That didn't seem to be a shot taken on purpose.

Or was it?

She didn't know what to think. Or what to believe. But something wasn't right here, and the longer Joe and Steele stayed inside, the more she felt certain this was a setup.

"Grayson?" She lifted her head to glance around. Grayson stood with his back to the passenger-side door.

He turned to glance at her briefly, before turning to scan the area again. "Stay put."

She swallowed a wave of frustration. She opened the door, bumping into him. There was just barely enough room for her to squeeze out of the vehicle to stand beside him.

"What are you doing?" Grayson's eyes widened in frank alarm. "Get back inside the car, Elly."

She ignored him. "I think this is a trap. I want you to call Joe, get him and Steele out of there."

"They're cops; they can take care of themselves." Grayson scowled. "Are you trying to get me fired? Joe will slice me to ribbons if you get hurt."

She grabbed Grayson's arm. "Listen, I was there when Kyle died. He tried to tell me something but could only say El. I think he wanted to warn me about Eloise. His wife!" She shook his arm with frustration. "Please call Joe. Hurry!"

Grayson looked torn but reluctantly reached for his phone. From the corner of her eye, she glimpsed a hint of movement. Without thinking it through, she threw herself at Grayson with enough force to knock him off balance. They tumbled to the ground, her landing on top of Grayson, covering him with her body as the sharp crack of gunfire rang out.

JOE WATCHED Eloise flinch at the sound of gunfire, the blood leeching from her face as if she herself had been struck. Alarm bells jangled loudly in the back of his mind.

From the moment he'd stepped inside the ranch house, he'd noticed something was off about Eloise.

She'd been nervous, avoiding direct eye contact. And now he knew why.

This was a trap! And he'd fallen for it.

"Steele, grab her!" Joe spun on his heel and bolted for the door. "Elly!" The shout was little more than a strangled sound.

Behind him, he heard the scuffle as Steele grabbed

Eloise. His gaze was focused on the SUV. It appeared empty.

Where were Elly and Grayson? He searched frantically for them and for the shooter.

Had they both been killed?

No, please, Lord Jesus, no! Don't take Elly from me!

His heart thundered in his chest as he ran toward the SUV in a crouch. At some level, he was aware that the other team members had come running at the sound of gunfire too. They had spread out, surrounding the SUV. But he'd gotten there first. He cautiously crab-walked around the back of the vehicle to reach the other side.

Two people were lying on the ground. It took him a minute to realize that Elly was on top of Grayson as if protecting him.

What in the world? It should have been the other way around!

Even as he crept closer, Grayson shook Elly off, causing her to slide onto the ground. In a quick movement, he rolled and crawled over her. When Elly grimaced as if in pain, he couldn't stand it.

"What happened? Is she hit?"

"I don't know," Grayson said, clearly upset and frustrated. "She plowed into me, catching me off guard just as the shot rang out."

For not being a cop, Elly sure had Finnegan cop instincts. It was both admirable and infuriating.

"I'm fine." Elly's strained voice belied her words. But at least she was able to talk. That was slightly reassuring.

"Where's the shooter?" He directed the question at Grayson or one of the other teammates, but it was Elly who answered.

"I saw movement from the light-green house behind us." Her voice was muffled. "I didn't see his face though."

"Backup has arrived," Brock shouted. "We'll find him!"

Joe was torn between checking Elly and searching for the shooter. With Grayson covering Elly, he forced himself to join the hunt.

This time, they could not let him get away.

Joe shot to his feet and sprinted toward the pale-green house, sweeping his gaze from side to side as he held his weapon ready. He slowed his pace upon reaching the building and took a moment to peek around the corner.

Nothing.

Gritting his teeth, he continued along the side of the green house, keeping a wary eye out for any sign of movement. Things had happened fast, yet he also knew the guy could have left the area immediately after taking the shot at Elly.

They had to find him. They just had to!

But as he came around the back side of the green house, he met up with Raelyn. She shook her head, indicating she hadn't seen the shooter either.

"Keep searching," he ordered, even though he felt certain they'd missed him. "I need to check back with Elly."

"Will do." Raelyn was joined by Brock, and the two team members fanned out to continue scouring the area. Joe noticed even more team members had arrived, Jina and Flynn were there too.

The entire tactical team had responded to his call for help. It was humbling, yet they still didn't have the shooter in custody.

And he feared they never would.

As he jogged back to the SUV, he saw Steele had dragged Eloise outside in handcuffs. It took all his willpower not to punch the woman who'd baited them into coming.

Setting Elly up to be shot and killed.

"Who is he?" He stormed toward Kyle's widow. "You know him, don't you? You're about to go down for aiding and abetting a murderer. Who is he?"

"Stop, please," Eloise begged. Her eyes filled with tears, but Joe couldn't come up with any sympathy for her. Not after this.

"Tell us who he is!" Joe was hanging onto his temper by a thread. "Right now!"

"Ashton James." The name was a choked sob. "He threatened to kill me. I had to call you to get you to come out to the house. I didn't have a choice!"

She had plenty of choices but hadn't made the right one. He nodded at Steele who pulled out his phone to get the name of Ashton James run through the system. "Where is he? Why is trying to kill Elly Finnegan?"

"I don't know," Eloise whimpered. "He's crazy. I told you he threatened to kill me if I didn't call you."

"Why would he do that?" Joe strove for patience. "How do you know him?"

Eloise squeezed her eyes together, tears leaking down her cheeks. He was about to grab her and shake the truth out of her, when she finally said, "Ash is a former boyfriend of mine. He's a cop from Detroit. But he used to work here, in Milwaukee as a police officer."

Detroit? "Then why is he here?"

"I—uh, started seeing him again recently, but then broke things off. I could tell he wasn't right in the head. To be honest, he seemed okay with it. He left me alone, and I figured that was the end of it." She gazed imploringly at him. "I never expected him to lash out like this, killing a bunch of innocent people at the parade. I swear to you, I had no idea that was his plan!"

Maybe she hadn't known that Ashton James was capable of something like that. But her excuse wasn't good enough. Not by a long shot.

"Why didn't you tell us about this after the Christmas parade shooting?" he demanded. "We could have had him in custody by now."

"He— I wasn't sure at first. I was supposed to be at the parade, too, but didn't go." Eloise was looking at each of the other teammates surrounding her as if seeking support. She didn't get any. "The sketch looked like him, but I was afraid that if I said anything, he'd come after me. Then I began to wonder if he'd planned to kill me that night too. Along with everyone else he'd taken out."

Joe remembered how angry Eloise had been that they hadn't gotten the shooter in custody. Had she really cowered inside of her house, waiting for them to find the guy? Without any help from her? Anger swirled in his chest, and it was all he could do not to unleash his fury on her.

He took a deep breath and let it out slowly. He couldn't change the past. But he wasn't going to let her get away with it either.

"Eloise Malaki, you're under arrest for aiding and abetting a murderer," he said flatly. "You have the right to remain silent, anything you say can and will be used against you in a court of law. You have the right . . ."

"I know my rights," she interrupted. "I was married to a cop. But this isn't my fault. I didn't know Ash would do this!"

Joe recited the rest of the Miranda warning, then added, "You knew this guy's name all this time and didn't tell us.

We could have had him in jail within hours if we'd had more information. If he's hurt anyone else, that's on you, Eloise. I hope you can live with yourself for the role you've played in this shooting." Full of disgust, he turned away, catching Elly's gaze. She looked upset at the interchange between them.

Of course, Elly with her soft heart would have some sympathy for the woman.

She was a better person than he was, that was for sure.

"Where is Ashton James now?" Steele demanded. "Where can we find him?"

"I—don't know. He mentioned staying at a trailer park, but I was never there." Eloise sounded subdued, as if the magnitude of her situation was finally hitting home. As it should. The public would not be happy to know there was a killer on the loose for almost three days because Eloise had kept her mouth shut.

Maybe the charges against her wouldn't stick, but that was the least of his worries. They still had to find this guy. And fast.

"Okay, we need to spread out and check all the trailer parks." He had no idea how many there were. "Call dispatch, have someone run them through the system."

"There's a trailer park about three miles from here," Raelyn said. "I know where it is, and it's close enough for him to use it as a hiding place. We need to get there ASAP."

"Go. Take several team members with you." Joe wanted to ride along, but when he glanced at Elly, he noticed the pained expression on her face. And the way she had one hand braced against the side of the SUV.

"Elly?" He rushed toward her. "What's wrong?"

"I'm fine." She didn't sound fine, just the opposite. From here, she appeared pale and fragile. "Just short of breath. Must be all the excitement and the rush of adrenaline."

"Are you sure you're not hit?" He ran his gaze over her, kicking himself for not examining her more closely.

"I didn't see any blood," Grayson said with a hint of defensiveness. "I checked."

Joe ignored him, still irrationally angry that Elly had been the one to jump on him, protecting a cop rather than the other way around. Then again, he knew Elly had amazing instincts. She'd saved his life, too, that fateful night.

Grayson didn't look happy at being caught off guard either.

"Hold still." He ran his fingers along the front of her vest but didn't find anything concerning.

Then he turned her around to check her back. Along her left side there was a gouge in the vest that had been made by a bullet.

"You were hit!" He hadn't meant to sound accusing, so he did his best to soften his tone. "I'm sorry, but you should have told me, you were struck by a bullet. You might have internal bleeding."

"I was?" She looked confused. "I didn't feel anything. Other than hitting the ground with Grayson."

Adrenaline could mask pain, so he believed her. "Okay, but what about now? Where do you hurt?"

"I, uh, maybe my ribs." She tried to reach over but froze and grimaced. "Um, yeah. That hurts."

Grayson looked upset. "I didn't realize. I'm sorry."

He managed to let his teammate off the hook. "She's talking, which is a good sign. Might have a couple of cracked or broken ribs from the impact of the slug. Call an ambulance, we need to get her to the hospital."

"Roger that." Grayson made the call as other officers converged on the area.

"I screwed up, Joe," Elly said in a low voice. "I should have considered that Kyle might have been the shooter's target. I thought Kyle wanted me to tell his wife he loved her."

"It's not your fault," he hastened to reassure her. "We all went down the path of believing the skaters had been the real targets."

"I think Kyle tried to warn me about Eloise," she continued as if he hadn't spoken. "Do you think he knew about her affair? About Ashton James? Maybe he even saw him?"

"I don't know." He wished Kyle had mentioned it to him.

"I keep running through those last few seconds in my mind. Kyle's expression was urgent, as if he really wanted to tell me something." She closed her eyes and shook her head. "It never occurred to me that he'd been hit on purpose."

"I didn't go there either, and I'm a trained cop." He wrapped his arm around her shoulder, offering his support. She gratefully leaned against him. "Don't beat yourself up, Elly. We'll get him."

"I wonder if Ash kept coming after me because he assumed Kyle had told me his name," she said half to herself. "I never could figure out why I was a threat."

"That theory only works if Kyle knew about the affair."

"Kyle did know about Ash," Eloise said.

He turned his head to stare at her. Another detail she'd failed to mention. "What makes you say that? What did he say to you?"

"Just that he saw Ash's name on my phone. And knew that we'd exchanged text messages." Eloise hunched her shoulders. "Kyle knew I used to date Ash when he was still working as a cop here in Milwaukee. I told him we were just friends, but I'm not sure if he believed me."

"Did Ash ever threaten to hurt Kyle?" he asked. "To kill him?"

"No." The way Eloise avoided his gaze wasn't reassuring. He had a feeling the guy had threatened Kyle. And that Eloise had kept her mouth shut about that too.

He hoped the DA would throw the book at her and made a mental note to ask Elly if either Bax Scala or Maddy Sinclair could take the case. Eloise needed to be held accountable for her actions. Or lack thereof.

What if Ash had succeeded in killing Elly? The mere thought had him breaking out in a cold sweat.

He loved her.

A weird calmness washed over him. Loving Elly felt right. And if he were honest, he'd admit he'd been fighting his feelings for her for months now.

Because of Rhy being his boss. And that wasn't fair to Elly. Or to him.

The arrival of the ambulance interrupted his thoughts. He almost groaned when he saw Colin jump out from the rig and run straight toward Elly.

"What happened? How badly are you hurt?" Colin asked.

"I'm fine. Just sore." Elly's smile looked strained.

There was no point in varnishing the truth. He stepped forward. "A bullet creased the back of Elly's vest. She's short of breath, and her ribs hurt."

"A bullet?" Colin narrowed his gaze. "You were supposed to protect her."

"He did," Elly insisted. "I'm standing here, aren't I?

Besides, I'm the one who got out of the car against Joe's and Grayson's advice."

Colin huffed but let it go. "Let's get you to the hospital."

Joe walked alongside. "I'm coming with you." When Colin looked as if he might argue, he added, "Ashton James, the shooter is still out there. We have officers searching for him now that we have a name and possible location. But I'm not leaving Elly's side until he's arrested."

Colin sighed. "Fine. I guess that's what Rhy would want."

"He would," Joe agreed.

"I'm right here," Elly said testily. "Does anyone care what I want?"

"Not really." Colin opened the back door of the rig. "Hold on. We need the gurney."

Joe stood to the side while Colin and a female paramedic pulled out the gurney, got Elly to lie down, then put her back inside the rig.

He jumped up beside her, taking her hand. He'd keep his promise to stick to Elly like glue.

And mentally prepared himself to face his boss's wrath over her injury.

CHAPTER FIFTEEN

Clinging to Joe's hand during the ambulance ride made Elly feel safe and secure. She knew Ashton James was still out there, but she was confident that the tactical team members would find him.

Her ribs hurt with every breath. She knew the injury was nothing compared to what so many others had suffered. Images from the Christmas shooting flashed in her mind. The dead skaters, Kyle, Lisa, and so many others.

"Take a deep breath," Colin said, after he'd placed an IV catheter in her arm.

"Can't, that hurts." She frowned.

"Try," her brother encouraged.

She breathed in, pain shooting through her ribs. "That's all you get," she managed.

"Okay." When Colin finished assessing her, he sat back. "Your vitals are stable, El. We'll know more once they run you through the CT scanner, but I don't see any sign of internal bleeding."

"That's good." She turned to gaze at Joe, telling herself

it was time to let the horror from the Christmas parade go. God had watched over them. They were alive and relatively unharmed. She couldn't ask for anything more.

"Are you okay?" Joe's blue eyes were full of concern.

"Yes." She couldn't help but smile, even as Colin eyed Joe with suspicion.

"We're coming up on Trinity Medical Center," the driver said.

"Understood," Colin replied. He patted her hand. "Don't worry, I'll let Rhy and the rest of the sibs know."

"Oh, please don't." She winced as the rig went over a bump. "I'm fine. There's no need to get the family all riled up."

The stubborn expression on Colin's face made her realize protesting was useless. She should be used to her older brothers' overprotectiveness by now.

When they arrived at the hospital, Colin and Joe wheeled her inside. She felt like a fraud because she wasn't hurt badly enough to need an ambulance.

When she was wheeled into a room, Alanna came rushing over. "Elly! I heard you were hurt! How are you?"

Elly inwardly groaned. This was what happened when you had eight older siblings working as first responders. "Fine, it's not bad."

"They won't let me be your nurse, but I'll be checking in frequently." Alanna moved back to allow a pretty dark-haired nurse to come in. "This is Dana Callahan, Mitch's wife. Dana, this is Elly Finnegan."

"I've heard so much about you," Dana said with a smile. "And we're all looking forward to the Christmas family reunion. Let's get you hooked up to our monitor." Dana arched a brow at Colin and Joe. "A little privacy please?"

"Of course." The tips of Joe's ears turned red as he hastened to get out of the room with Colin on his heels.

Once the bullet-resistant vest and her clothes were removed, Dana put her in a hospital gown. Shortly thereafter, a doctor came in. Not Colin's wife, Faye, probably for the same reason Alanna couldn't be her nurse, but an older guy by the name of Dr. Willis who had kind eyes.

Things happened quickly after that. She was whisked down the hall to the radiology department for the promised CT scan. Moving from the bed to the table hurt far more than she'd expected.

"This shouldn't take too long," the tech assured her.

"I'm fine." She was tempted to write the words in indelible ink on her forehead so she wouldn't need to keep repeating herself.

Twenty minutes later, Elly was transferred back to the gurney and wheeled into her room. The tech assured her someone would be in shortly. Being alone, even briefly, was nice. She couldn't take a deep breath without wanting to cry, but the nightmare was over.

Her body and her mind would heal. Her heart? She couldn't hide the wave of sadness. Joe had protected her for her brother's sake. And because she'd been like a sister to him.

Loving Joe was incredibly easy. Letting him go would be one of the most difficult things she'd ever done.

"Elly?" She turned to see Joe hovering in the doorway.

"Hey." She lifted her hand. "Please don't ask how I'm doing. I feel like I've answered that a hundred times already."

"Okay, I won't ask." His intense gaze held hers. "I just heard from Raelyn. They found the trailer Ashton was living in, along with a detailed sketch of the parade route and his assault weapon, but there's no sign of him. They're canvassing the neighbors now. And, of course, we've issued a BOLO for him with his Detroit driver's license photo. He'll be caught soon enough."

"I'm sure he will." She honestly wasn't worried. Having the evil man's name was a game changer. He'd no longer be able to hide in anonymity.

The sound of loud beeping came from another room. Hospital staff, including Alanna, scurried past her doorway to attend to the patient's needs.

Joe stepped out to glance toward the commotion. A tall man wearing hospital scrubs, a paper hat over his head, and a face mask loomed behind him. The guy turned and looked directly at her.

The shooter! "Ashton's behind you!"

The guy froze momentarily just as Joe spun toward him. Ashton had a good two inches on Joe, but that didn't seem to matter. Joe's fist shot out, catching the shooter beneath his chin. Ashton's head snapped back, but he didn't go down.

Elly watched in horror as Ashton pulled his hand from his scrub pocket, revealing a small gun. "Look out!"

Before the warning left her mouth, Joe threw himself at Ashton, knocking him off his feet. The two men tumbled down, and she thought she heard the clatter of a gun hitting the floor. Elly swung herself upright, ignoring the pain as she stood and moved toward the door.

Colin jumped into the fray, helping Joe get control of the guy. Elly saw the gun on the floor and used her bare foot to kick it out of reach. Then she stood helplessly watching as Ashton and Joe exchanged fierce blows as Colin did his best to grab Ashton's arms.

Suddenly Brady, Rhy, and Tarin were there too. She

sagged against the doorframe in relief as her brothers grabbed Ashton and hauled him upward. Rhy wrenched Ashton's arms behind his back as Tarin pulled the face mask and cap off, revealing his features. Blood ran from his nose, and his lip was bleeding too.

Ashton muttered a curse, then clamped his mouth shut. Hatred burned from his eyes. She glared right back, satisfied that he'd never hurt anyone, ever again.

She forced herself to turn away. Noticing Joe's battered face, she moved toward him. "Oh, Joe, that looks painful."

"I'm okay." Joe swiped his hand over his face to get rid of the blood. Then he looked at her. "How did you recognize him?"

"His eyes." She managed a wan smile as Tarin and Brady hauled Ashton away. "I told you before that I'd know him when I saw him. Even with the mask and hat covering his features, I recognized his eyes."

"You're good, sis," Rhy said with admiration.

"Thanks." She reached out to grasp Joe's arm. "Your poor face needs medical attention."

"Nah, I've had worse." Joe slipped his arm around her waist. "You, on the other hand, need to get back into bed."

She reluctantly allowed him to help her onto the gurney. Mostly because she still didn't know the results of the CT scan. It didn't feel as if she was bleeding internally, but since she'd never been struck by a bullet while wearing a vest, she had no way of knowing for sure.

"Kingsley," Rhy said, coming into the room.

Joe turned and faced her brother. "I know what you're going to say. It's my fault. I take full responsibility for Elly getting hurt."

Rhy arched a brow and clapped him on the back. "That

wasn't what I was going to say. You did good work here. I heard from Brady, Quinn, and Tarin how determined you were to keep Elly safe. I appreciate everything you've done for her."

Joe scowled. "It's still my fault she was hurt."

"We have security searching the area to figure out how the shooter got his weapon past the metal detector. We believe he assaulted a staff member and stole his ID." Rhy looked grim. "Sounds like they haven't implemented scanning employees the way I'd hoped."

She remembered when Alanna had almost been shot by an employee with a gun. Maybe this latest incident would change the policy.

"Excuse me." Dr. Willis tapped on the door. "I need to speak with Ms. Finnegan about the results of her CT scan." He frowned, and added, "Privately."

"Go ahead." Elly waved a hand. "Joe and Rhy can hear this."

Willis eyed the two men warily, then shrugged. "Okay. The good news is that you don't have any internal bleeding. However, you do have two cracked ribs and severe bruising. You're going to be sore for the next six to eight weeks, I'm afraid. You'll need to avoid heavy lifting during that time frame."

"What about my job?" Elly asked. "I'm an EMT."

"Sorry." Dr. Willis shook his head. "You'll have to take a medical leave of absence. I'll give you a note with your lifting restriction to take to your employer."

"Does she need to stay overnight?" Joe asked.

"No, she can go home. Ribs heal on their own over time. I'll put through the discharge order now." Willis ducked out of the room.

"How exactly did Elly get shot?" Rhy asked.

Joe rubbed the back of his neck. "She caught a glimpse of the shooter and threw herself on top of Grayson to protect him."

"Really?" Rhy turned to face her. "Sounds like you would have made a good cop after all."

"No thanks." She didn't want to be a cop, but for the first time in years, she felt as if she truly belonged to the Finnegan family. That maybe she wasn't just the youngest, oops baby. Going through all of this gave her a new appreciation for her siblings' respective careers.

"Well, now that you can't be an EMT, you can take your time off to think about what you really want to do," Rhy said. "We know you don't like your current job."

"What do you mean?" She frowned. Had she really been that transparent? She'd thought she'd done a good job of hiding her aversion to blood.

"Come on, sis," Rhy said gently. "It was obvious you didn't like your career."

"Maybe she was tentative before mostly because she hated the sight of blood," Joe said. "But you need to know she handled the scene of the shooting like a real pro. She darted into the line of fire to get a young boy to the rig, then she took her first aid from one victim to the other providing care along the way. She did a great job triaging too. And she saved my life."

Joe's compliment warmed her heart. Although she'd wished he hadn't let her secret out.

"Who goes into the EMT program if they can't stand the sight of blood?" Rhy threw up his hands. "You should have told me."

"I'm over it." She waved a hand. "That was one benefit to being at the Christmas parade."

"Ah, Elly." Rhy sighed. "You don't have to prove yourself to us. We only want you to be happy."

"I know." Her eyes misted with tears. "Thanks, Rhy. That means a lot."

Joe cleared his throat. "I should go."

"No, wait." Elly didn't want him to leave. Thankfully, Rhy turned to join the rest of the siblings who were still congregated in the hallway outside her room. Hiding a wince, she sat up and swung her legs over the edge of the gurney.

"What are you doing?" Joe looked alarmed.

"Standing. The doctor only mentioned a lifting restriction. I can stand and walk, Joe." She tamped back a surge of frustration. Moving closer, she slipped her arm around his waist. "I'm so glad you're here."

"Me too." Joe gave her a hug. "I'm glad I was able to catch Ashton off guard long enough to take him down."

"That was great, but I was referring to having you here. Supporting me." She longed to kiss him. "Will you come to the homestead on Christmas Day?" She looked up at him. "We're having a Callahan and Finnegan family reunion."

"Sounds like a day best spent with family," Joe murmured. He hugged her, then took a step back. "I have to go. Your family will take you home."

"But . . ." It was no use. Joe slipped out the door, leaving her alone.

FORCING himself to leave Elly wasn't easy. But most of the Finnegan clan was there and were more than capable of looking after her.

Joe had been surprised at how easily Rhy had let him off

the hook over Elly's injuries. He'd fully expected to get hammered by his boss, but the eldest Finnegan had taken the events in stride. No doubt, finding Elly awake, alert, and able to communicate had helped.

He'd barely stepped outside when his phone rang. Expecting to hear from someone on the team, he was surprised to recognize Rhy's number. "What's up? Did you need something?"

"Stay put, I'm coming." Rhy ended the call but jogged out of the emergency department less than a minute later.

Was this the moment Rhy would rake him over the coals? He straightened his shoulders. "What's wrong?"

"I'm still worried about Elly," Rhy said. "You've been with her the most over these past few days. Do you think she's suffering from PTSD?"

He hesitated, then decided lying to his boss wasn't smart. "Yes, she's had some nightmares. The way anyone would. I really think this is something you should discuss with Elly."

Rhy's brown eyes narrowed. "I'm asking you."

"Look, I get she's the youngest and that you've spent the past eleven years protecting her," Joe said. "But Elly is a beautiful, smart, strong, and capable woman. She's not a kid."

"Sounds like you admire her."

"I love her." He hadn't meant to blurt out the truth like that.

"Joe! Wait." Elly was dressed in her regular clothes, pressing a hand against her left side as she hobbled toward them. "Don't go. I need to talk to you."

Rhy took a step back and crossed his arms over his chest. Joe noticed he didn't look happy, but he hadn't gotten punched in the nose yet either.

He found that slightly reassuring.

"Take a hike, Rhy." Elly came over to stand beside him.

Rhy laughed. "Yeah, that's not happening."

"Yes, it is." Elly took a step toward him, holding his gaze. "I'm sick and tired of you trying to intimidate guys I might be interested in. Enough is enough. I'm almost twenty-five years old. I don't need your protection anymore. I can handle my personal life all on my own."

"I don't try to intimidate your boyfriends," he protested.

"Yes, you do. Cleaning your service weapon in the living room on prom night for both me and Alanna. Running every guy I ever dated through the simple case search to find out if he has a criminal record." She huffed, then winced and grabbed her ribs. "Back off, Rhy. I mean it."

Joe wanted to smile at the way Elly stood up to her brother.

"I taught you and Alanna to do a simple case search on potential boyfriends to help you out," Rhy said mildly. "Not as an intimidation tactic."

Elly looked up to the dark sky, then said, "Rhy, if you really care about me, you'll give me and Joe some privacy." She didn't back down.

"It's okay, Rhy," he said. "You know Elly is safe with me."

"Do I?" Rhy's gaze bored into his. "Okay, fine. You get five minutes."

"I'll take as much time as I want," Elly shot back.

Rhy didn't answer, but he did go back inside the emergency department. Elly turned back to him, looking adorably frustrated.

"What did you want to talk about?" he asked.

"You. Me. Us." She frowned. "Joe, I care about you. A lot."

His heart swelled with hope. "I care about you too, Elly."

"Then why are you leaving like this?" She stepped closer, resting the palm of her hand on the center of his chest. He couldn't help reaching up to cover it with his own. "Why won't you come to our Christmas party?"

"Family reunion," he corrected. "Elly, I'm not family."

"You are to me." The words were spoken so softly he thought he hadn't heard them clearly. "I love you, Joe."

Her declaration knocked him off balance. "Elly, we've been through a difficult and dangerous time. Your feelings will likely change . . ."

"No, they won't," she interrupted. "Because I've cared about you for months now. Long before the Christmas parade shooting. I was trying to get up enough nerve to ask you out."

Really? She'd wanted to ask him out? He searched her gaze. "I don't know what to say."

The light in her eyes dimmed. "It's okay, Joe. I can understand if you don't feel the same way."

"I do," he quickly interjected. Then he laughed and carefully drew her into his arms. "Elly, I already told Rhy I've fallen in love with you. And the good news is that he didn't take a swing at me like I half expected."

"Is that why he wouldn't leave us alone?" Elly rolled her eyes. "Older brothers are a pain."

"I heard that," a male voice called from the darkness.

Over Elly's shoulder, he watched Rhy emerge from the shadows. Joe wondered if his boss had changed his mind about raking him over the coals.

"Go away, Rhy," Elly said without looking at him. "We're busy."

"Yeah, I can see that." Rhy stepped closer. "Sounds like the two of you are perfect for each other."

Joe eyed him warily. "Does that mean you're giving us your blessing?"

"Yeah, it does. Elly deserves a guy like you, Kingsley." Rhy lightly punched him in the arm. "Like I said before, though, don't hurt her."

"Never," he promised.

Rhy nodded and turned away, heading into the building for real this time.

"Ignore him," Elly said, then grinned. "Except for the part where we're perfect for each other."

That made him laugh. "I can appreciate how Rhy and your other siblings care about you, Elly." He gazed into her eyes. "But I love you for the woman you are. Strong, brave, smart, and courageous." He paused, then added, "Let's not forget stubborn. Very, very stubborn."

"I love you too, Joe." She hugged him. "It takes a strong man to take on the Finnegan family."

"The Finnegans don't scare me," he murmured, then lowered his mouth to capture hers in a deep kiss.

For long moments, he cradled her close, basking in the glow of Elly's love. He broke off the kiss when she shivered in the chilly breeze.

"Let's get you back inside," he said. "It's cold out here."

"Okay, but you haven't answered my question." She kept her arm around his waist as they headed inside.

"What question?" Kissing her had robbed him of all thought. Especially when all he wanted was to kiss her again.

"Will you please come to our Christmas family reunion this upcoming Saturday?" She tightened her arm around his waist. "I love you, Joe. And I want you to be there as we celebrate the birth of Jesus with the entire extended family."

"Yes, Elly, I'd be honored." He'd do anything for her, even facing the entire Finnegan and Callahan family in one fell swoop.

Anything, for love.

EPILOGUE

Christmas Day . . .

Elly glanced around the Finnegan homestead one last time, satisfied with the Christmas decorations. The entire Finnegan family was there, and the Callahans would be arriving at any moment.

"What else do you need?" Joe asked, coming over to stand beside her. He'd been overly protective all morning as she'd made preparations for the reunion, barely letting her lift a plate or cup. He also stole a kiss or two under the mistletoe.

She wasn't complaining. She'd seen him often this past week and loved him more every day.

"How are things outside?" Elly asked.

"Tent is in place, tables are set up, and warmers are on. It's not bad out there," Joe admitted. "Thankfully, the weather today is milder than usual."

"Great. The food is all set in the kitchen." She wanted the entire family to gather in the main living area at first but knew they wouldn't be able to sit inside comfortably for long. The house wasn't that big.

The doorbell rang. Elly grinned at Joe before hurrying over to answer it.

"Hi, Marc, oh, you must be Kari," Elly greeted the oldest Callahan sibling and his wife. "And Max and Maggie," she added, smiling at the shy five-year-old boy and the three-year-old girl.

"Elly, it's wonderful of you to have us over." Kari placed a hand on her round, pregnant belly. "We've been looking forward to this reunion for months."

"Me too." Elly gestured for them to come inside. "Please, make yourselves at home. Oh, and this is Joe Kingsley." She hesitated, then added self-consciously, "My boyfriend."

Joe led them to the rest of the family members, where more introductions were made. Most of the siblings knew the Callahans from the way they'd helped out over the past year, but their spouses and children were new to the group.

Matthew and Lacy were the next to arrive, with their son Rory and a brand-new baby girl named Olivia. Matt's K-9 Duchess trotted straight to Caleb, pressing her nose against the little boy she'd help find months ago.

"Duchess!" Caleb threw his arms around the German shepherd's neck.

"We're going to have to get a dog," Brady murmured to Grace.

Twenty minutes later, the entire family was gathered together in the great room. Even the matriarch of the Callahan family, Maggie O'Hare and her new husband, Ian O'Hare, had come to the event. The four pregnant women, Kari Callahan, Joy Finnegan, Maddy Sinclair, and Kyleigh Finnegan were all seated on the sofa while everyone else stood.

The numerous kids were already becoming fast friends.

Brady and Grace's son Caleb, Aiden and Shelby's daughter Eva, and their newest member of the family, Colleen, were the only kids on the Finnegan side. The Callahans were way ahead of them on that front. Miles and Paige had two kids, a daughter Abby and their son, Adam. Then there were Marc and Kari's two kids, Max and Maggie, Dana and Mitch had Simon and Trina, Mike and Shayla had Brodie and Carly, Matthew and Lacy had their son Rory and a newborn baby named Olivia who was born last month just like Rhy's daughter, Colleen. Lastly, Maddy and Noah Sinclair had a three-year-old son named Brian, and Maddy was expecting again. Between the adults, the kids, and Duchess, the house was packed.

"It's chaos in here," Joe whispered.

No joke. But she still loved it. The family members meshed as if they'd known each other their entire lives rather than reconnecting this past year.

"Excuse me, everyone, could I have your attention?" Elly shouted to be heard above the din. When the voices didn't quiet, Joe let out a loud whistle. The group fell silent. She chuckled. "Thanks, Joe. Okay, I have an announcement to make about our family tree."

"You do?" Maddy looked intrigued. "Why didn't you tell me?"

"I wanted to wait until we were all together." Elly lifted a small leather-bound notebook with yellowed pages from the coffee table. "I found Grandma Josephine's diary in the attic. I know what happened between our grandmothers all those years ago."

An expectant hush cloaked the room. Finally, Rhy said, "Don't keep us in suspense, Elly. What does it say?"

"Grandma Josephine O'Brady, that was her maiden name, wrote about how she was sent away to help a family with three small children," Elly began. "I guess this was a common practice back then. Older siblings were offered to other families to help during times of need. Sort of like free babysitting and housekeeping services. According to her diary, Grandma Josephine wasn't happy about the decision but did her duty as requested."

"Okay, but why did she break off communications with her own sister, our Grandma Margaret?" Maddy asked. "I don't understand."

"Grandma Josephine ran away from the family after the father of the children tried to force himself on her. He didn't succeed," she hastily added, "because she hit him with a cast-iron skillet, but she was too afraid to go back home, knowing her leaving so abruptly would bring shame to the family. And also, there was some resentment on her part because they sent her to stay with the family in the first place."

"That poor woman," Shayla murmured.

"Then what happened?" Mike asked.

"Grandma Josephine made her way to the city where she worked at a boarding house. And that's where she met our grandfather, Michael Daley. They only had one daughter, our mother, Colleen who then married our dad." She smiled. "Grandma Josephine had a good life despite never contacting her family again. Which is sad, I know." She gazed around the room. "But look at us now. Here we are, three generations sitting in this room dating all the way back to our mutual great-grandparents, Thomas and Catherine O'Brady. I know our grandmothers Josephine and Margaret are in heaven looking down on us, thrilled to know we've been reunited."

"That's amazing," Marc said. "I'm really glad you and

Maddy did the DNA testing, Elly. Without you two starting this, we wouldn't be gathered here today."

"Yes, that's true." Elly grinned at her cousin Maddy. "And it's obvious that being first responders is in our blood."

"No lie," Colin said. "It's incredible how our similar our respective careers are too." He frowned. "Except for you, Maddy. None of the Finnegans became a lawyer."

"But I married one," Kyleigh pointed out, smiling at her husband, Bax.

"Well, thank you, Elly, for bringing us together and for solving our family mystery," Maggie O'Hare said. "I knew my mother had lost contact with her sister, Josephine, but even I didn't know all of this. I'd like to review that diary in more detail if you don't mind."

"Of course not." Elly crossed over to hand the diary to the eldest member of the Callahan clan. "I'm so glad you and Ian could join us today."

"Ah, there's one more thing before we dig into the meal," Joe said as he returned to stand beside her. "If I could have your attention for one brief minute?"

The group gazed at him expectantly. Elly caught a glint of satisfaction in Rhy's eyes, seconds before Joe turned to her. Then he went down on one knee and held out an engagement ring. "Elly, I love you with all my heart. Will you please marry me?"

She gaped in shock. When had he planned this? Then she smiled and blinked back tears of happiness. "Yes, Joe. I can't wait to marry you!" She let him slide the ring on her finger, then threw herself into his arms, ignoring the twinge of pain from her cracked ribs.

The entire family, including the youngest generation of kids who may or may not have understood exactly what they were excited about, burst into applause.

"Hey, you're moving a little fast, Joe, don't you think?" Colin asked with a frown. "You and Elly only began seeing each other over this past week. Who do you think you are, Speedy Gonzales from the old cartoon?"

"Gonzo!" Brady declared. "That's Joe's new nickname. Gonzo!"

"Gonzo, Gonzo, Gonzo," Brodie and Caleb began chanting.

"I don't get it," Maddy said with a frown. "Why does he need a nickname? Do all the Finnegan spouses have nicknames?"

"No, only the men our sisters fall in love with get nicknames," Quinn said. "It's a tradition."

"Yeah, one you guys made up when I fell in love with Bax, calling him Penguin," Kyleigh groused. "Just because he wore a tux to Rhy and Devon's wedding."

"Ah, but did you know that penguins can swim at speeds of ten miles per hour?" Bax asked. "They are truly remarkable flightless aquatic birds."

"You sound like an encyclopedia," Sami complained. "I'm glad I didn't get a nickname."

Reed puffed out his chest. "Just call me Clark. Clark Kent. A.k.a. Superman." He smirked. "That's better than Gonzo and Penguin." He lifted his arms to the ceiling in a touchdown formation. "I win!"

"Oh, for Pete's sake," Elly muttered, rolling her eyes. "I'm sorry, Joe."

"I'm not." Joe kissed her. "I love you, Elly. Thanks for making me the happiest man on earth."

"I love you so much," she whispered. "Kiss me again."

He laughed and kissed her again. Then he turned to face her family. "Did any of you hear the story about how Elly brought a stray dog home that turned out to be a coyote pup? She hid it from Rhy for three days before he found out."

"No way," Paige exclaimed. "That's scary!"

"You have no idea," Rhy said on a sigh. "Especially since the little bugger bit her. I was worried she'd get rabies from that thing."

The rest of her siblings brought up other stories until the entire group was laughing so hard they were crying.

Elly couldn't complain since they were true. And she didn't really mind. All that mattered was that they were here together on this beautiful Christmas Day.

And that God had blessed her with a wonderful man who was a perfect fit with the Finnegan family.

THANKS so much for reading the exciting conclusion of my Finnegan First Responders series. I truly hope you enjoyed Joe and Elly's story along with the Finnegan and Callahan family reunion. You may be interested in my new Oath of Honor series. Each member of Rhy and Joe's tactical team will get their own happily ever after. Are you ready for Steele and Harper's story in *Steele*? Click Here!

DEAR READER

Thanks so much for reading my Finnegan First Responder series. I'm truly blessed to have wonderful readers like you. And I've had so much fun bringing the Callahans and Finnegans together for a Christmas family reunion!

I'm kicking off my next series in January featuring the members of Rhy's tactical team. You met many of them in Elly and Joe's story. *Steele* will be the first book in my Oath of Honor series. I will have *Steele* available on my website for a full month before it's available anywhere else. Don't forget, you can purchase eBooks or audiobooks directly from my website will receive a 15% discount by using the code **LauraScott15**.

I adore hearing from my readers! I can be found through my website at https://www.laurascottbooks.com, via Facebook at https://www.facebook.com/LauraScott Books, Instagram at https://www.instagram.com/laurascott books/, and Twitter https://twitter.com/laurascottbooks. Please take a moment to subscribe to my YouTube channel at youtube.com/@LauraScottBooks-wr1xl?sub_confirmation=1. Also, take a moment to sign up for my monthly newsletter to learn about my new book releases! All subscribers receive a free novella not available for purchase on any platform.

Until next time,
Laura Scott
PS: Read on for a sneak peek of *Steele*.

STEELE

Chapter One

Harper Crane huddled in her winter coat as she hurried along the snowy sidewalk. She absolutely hated parking in downtown Milwaukee, especially in January, but it couldn't be helped. Her role as a legal assistant to Gibson and Roberts law offices meant showing up at the high-rise building four days a week. Her boss, Trent Gibson, let her work from home every Friday, unless he had depositions scheduled in one of the conference rooms.

Shivering, she increased her pace. The surface parking lot she used charged ten bucks a day. The structures were more than twice that amount, so she ducked her head against the wind and pushed forward. The office building was only five blocks away.

She was so busy watching her feet to make sure she didn't slip and fall she didn't pay much attention to the vehicle coming up beside her. Even when it idled in the road, she didn't think much about it. When the back passenger door opened and a man stepped out, her instincts finally kicked in.

Danger!

A hard hand grabbed her arm. No! She tried to tug out of his grip, her stupid office flats slipping on the icy pavement.

She opened her mouth to scream, but he ruthlessly clamped his other hand over his mouth and began dragging her toward the car.

A silent scream lodged in her throat as she struggled against his grip. This couldn't be happening. She couldn't allow him to get her into the car!

"Police! Get your hands where I can see them!"

The shout came from her left, and the assailant instantly let her go, shoving her backward, then diving into the back seat of the car. The driver hit the gas and careened away from the curb, tires squealing and horns blaring as he rounded the corner and disappeared. A cop chased after the vehicle, but then stopped and turned to jog back toward her.

Harper landed hard on her backside, her arms instinctively curling around her pregnant belly. She couldn't breathe, couldn't do anything but stare up in horror as uniformed police officers rushed to her side.

"Ms. Crane? Are you okay?" The fact that the dark-haired cop knew her name wasn't reassuring. She stared up into his blue eyes, trying to comprehend what had transpired.

"We need to get her up," the other officer said.

"Okay, easy now." The cop with dark hair and blue eyes slid his arm behind her shoulders. With the help of both men, she managed to get back on her feet. Her body was sore, especially her tailbone, but she relaxed when she felt her baby moving. Should she go to the hospital to be checked out? She wasn't sure that was necessary but didn't want to take any chances with her baby's life.

"Can you tell us what happened?" Her gaze landed on the dark-haired cop's name tag. His last name was Delaney. The other officer's name tag read Greer.

"I—have no idea." She pushed the words through her tight throat. "Out of nowhere, this guy came out of the car and tried to kidnap me."

The two cops exchanged a glance. Delaney nodded. "Yes, ma'am, we know that much. Did you recognize the man who grabbed you? Did he say anything?"

"Why would I recognize him?" None of this seemed real, although clearly it was. If not for these two men showing up in the nick of time . . . she swallowed hard. "No, he didn't look familiar." She thought back to those tense moments when she'd belatedly realized what the guy's intent was. "He didn't say anything. Just grabbed me, clapped his hand over my mouth, and dragged me toward the car . . ." She broke off, swallowing hard.

"Okay, that's fine. We had to ask." Officer Delaney spoke in a soothing voice. "Brock, did you get his license plate number?"

"Yeah. Sent it to dispatch to issue a BOLO on the vehicle," Officer Greer said.

"We'd like you to come down to the precinct to look at some mug shots." Officer Delaney smiled reassuringly. "I'm sure your boss won't mind. We can call the law office from the squad, explain that you need some time off."

Her boss at the law office? Time off? The hairs on the back of her neck rose in alarm. These cops knew her name. They knew where she worked. They probably knew more about her personal life than her boss did.

Realization sank deep. They hadn't just gotten here so

quickly by chance. She narrowed her gaze at Officer Delaney. "You were following me? Watching me and following me? Why?"

Delaney held her gaze for a long moment. "It's best if you come with us. We can discuss this in more detail at the precinct."

Somehow, she sensed it would be better for them—not her—to go along with the plan. Yet someone had tried to kidnap her. This—she didn't understand any of this. Her shoulders slumped, and she slowly shook her head. "This is about Jake, isn't it?"

"You tell us." Officer Greer arched his brow.

She scowled. She didn't like him. Either of them. They'd been watching her. Waiting for something bad to happen. And it had!

With an abrupt move, she twisted away from Officer Delaney and walked away. She wasn't going anywhere with them.

"Ms. Crane," Delaney called her name as he quickly caught up with her. "You can't just pretend this didn't happen. Don't you realize you're in danger?"

"Why?" She spun to face him. He was so close her belly bumped into him. He hastily stepped back as if burned. "I don't understand. My ex-husband is dead! He can't testify. There's no reason for anyone to come after me. To try and kidnap me!"

"Clearly, someone associated with your ex-husband wants something from you." His placating tone grated on her nerves. "Please, come with us to the precinct. We really need to talk."

Her baby kicked again, and she put a hand to her abdomen beneath her coat to soothe her baby. She was just over seven months pregnant. Stress wasn't good for either of them.

"Fine." She turned to face him. "But you better be prepared to share what you know too. I want answers, Officer Delaney, especially if me and my baby are truly in danger."

The cop's gaze dropped momentarily to her abdomen, before bouncing back up to meet hers. "I understand."

Did he? She wasn't convinced. Yet she didn't have much of a choice but to go along with them. Not if she wanted to understand exactly what was going on.

She reluctantly allowed Delaney to escort her back to where his partner, Greer, waited, hoping and praying she wouldn't regret this.

STEELE COULDN'T BELIEVE Jacob Feldman's pregnant ex-wife had almost been snatched right under their noses. The near miss would earn them a scowl from their bosses, Lieutenant Joe Kingsley and Captain Rhy Finnegan. Both guys were fair and decent men, but they also held high standards.

He would take full responsibility for the incident. He and Brock had been watching her from a distance. He hadn't anticipated these guys would try to grab her during daylight hours, early in the morning no less.

He hated knowing Harper was pregnant and in danger. She was right, none of this was her fault.

He was certain the actions of her ex-husband had dragged her into this mess. What Harper didn't know was that Feldman wasn't killed in prison the way she'd been told.

No, the weasel had decided to testify against his coconspirators, so his death had been faked. Easily enough to do after he'd gotten beat up in prison bad enough to require a trip to the hospital. He was currently being held in a safe house down in Chicago. The truth would be revealed when they got closer to trial.

Someone else obviously knew Feldman was still alive. Maybe they'd even decided to abduct Harper as leverage against Feldman, hoping to get the guy to change his mind about testifying against the big boss, Tommy Grotto.

Either that or someone believed Harper knew more about Feldman's illegal activities than she'd let on.

Considering the way Harper had filed for divorce exactly twenty-four hours *before* Jacob Feldman was arrested, he felt certain she had discovered key information related to his illegal activities.

A theory that seemed to have been the motive behind the abduction attempt.

Glancing at her in the rearview mirror, Steele took note of the way she stared out through the window without saying a word.

"Did you want us to call your boss?" he asked, breaking the silence.

Her jaw tightened, but she shook her head and pulled her phone from her purse. "I'll do it."

He and Brock exchanged a glance as she made the call, explaining to her boss, Attorney Trent Gibson, about how she'd been attacked and was being taken to the police station for questioning.

"I promise I'm fine and so is the baby," she said. "I don't know how long this will take, though."

Another silence as she listened to whatever her boss was saying.

"Okay, thanks, Trent. I appreciate that. I'll let you know." She lowered the phone, then asked, "Does my boss know about you two following me?"

"No, we've never met him." He held her gaze in the rearview mirror. "We only know that he's your boss."

"Yeah, sure." Her tone indicated she didn't believe him.

Brock shrugged and looked away. Steele could tell that his fellow teammate didn't trust Harper Crane any more than she trusted them.

He pulled into the parking lot of the third district police station, then threw the gearshift into park. He pushed out from behind the wheel, then quickly jumped out to open the back passenger door for Harper, knowing she couldn't get out of the caged area on her own.

"Be careful," he warned, taking her elbow. "It's slippery."

She gave a curt nod and allowed him to escort her inside. Brock followed behind, covering her back without being asked.

Whoever had tried to grab Harper could easily try again. A fact he wasn't sure she really appreciated.

"This way." He steered her through the maze of cubicles to one of the interview rooms. "Have a seat."

She did, then crossed her arms over her chest. "How long is this going to take?"

He stifled a sigh, dropping into a chair across from her. "Ms. Crane, we need to understand how much you knew about your husband's business dealings."

"Ex-husband." She held his gaze for a long moment, then added, "I didn't know anything. I had no idea he was about to be arrested."

He didn't believe it. "So you're saying it was just a coincidence that he was arrested twenty-four hours after you filed for divorce?"

A flicker of uncertainty darkened her green eyes, but then she nodded. "Yes. I—he'd changed. He became withdrawn, terse, angry, and verbally abusive." She dropped her hands to her pregnant belly. "He'd morphed into a completely different person from the man I'd married two years ago."

Steele swallowed a sigh. He'd hoped she'd be more forthcoming after nearly being kidnapped off the street. "Those guys tried to grab you for a reason, Ms. Crane. Have you considered what might have happened if we hadn't been there?"

"Yes." Her voice was a whisper. She closed her eyes for a moment, then lifted her gaze to his. She was stunning with her long blond hair and bright-green eyes. And for a moment, he had to wonder if the abduction was for another, more sinister reason. Sex traffickers didn't normally target pregnant women, but it was possible they hadn't known about her condition. If he hadn't been watching her move around inside her apartment, he might not have noticed either. Her winter coat was big enough to cover her rounded belly.

"I neglected to thank you and Officer Greer for saving me," she said, as if having come to the realization that arguing with them wasn't going to work in her favor. She frowned. "Although I have to admit it's more than a little disconcerting to realize you've been watching me, following my movements."

He wasn't going to apologize for keeping an eye on her. They'd run out of leads and had decided to keep tabs on Feldman's ex-wife. He was secretly glad they had. "You know this attempt to grab you must be related to your ex-husband. We need you to tell us everything you know to find the men responsible." He paused, then added, "Before they try again."

"Again?" She paled. "You think they will?"

"Ma'am, you need to come clean right now," Brock said, betraying his impatience. "Tell us who grabbed you and why."

"I don't know!" Harper's voice held anguish as she slapped her hands on the metal table. "If I did, I'd tell you! Don't you think I'd do whatever necessary to protect my baby?"

Steele frowned at Brock, silently warning him to back off.

"Yes, I know you would protect your baby in any way possible," he hastened to reassure her. "But, Ms. Crane, we need you to think back. There may be something your husband said that may help us now."

"Ex-husband!" she shouted. Then her face crumpled. "This isn't my fault. I didn't do anything illegal."

"No, you didn't." He reached across the table to take her hand. "I'm sorry you're having to deal with this, but it's going to be difficult to protect you if we don't know who is behind this attempted kidnapping."

She pulled away, swiped at her face, then met his gaze. "I gave the names of my ex-husband's friends to the police when he was arrested. I barely saw Jake for those two weeks before I moved out. I—he caught me leaving with the last box and forced me to sleep with him." Her voice hiccupped, and his heart squeezed at hearing what she'd suffered. "Then he got a call and left the house saying something about how he'd be there right away. I took it as a sign from God and got out of there as quickly as possible."

"And you don't know who called him? Or what the call was about?" he gently pressed.

"No. I was pretty upset, as you can imagine." She blinked tears from her eyes and swiped at her face again. "I thought the call might be from Starkey. Ellis Starkey is one of his closest friends. But I can't say for sure."

They knew about Ellis Starkey who had seemingly disappeared off the face of the earth, either hiding or dead, and had been hoping for more. "You didn't know about the guns he was buying and selling?"

"No." She held his gaze. "I hate guns, and Jake knew that. He would never have told me he was buying and selling them." She put a hand on her abdomen again. "If I had known, I would have left him much earlier."

She was probably thinking that if she had done that, she wouldn't be pregnant now. He wondered how she felt about that, then decided it was none of his business.

Brock rose to his feet and headed for the door. "I need air," he muttered.

Steele understood his buddy's anger and frustration. They were all running low on sleep since the most recent raid on a warehouse in Ravenswood that had been coordinated by the ATF with backup from their tactical team had ended in a major gunfight where too many of the bad guys had managed to escape. Their teammate Flynn had been nicked by a bullet, but thankfully, they had killed three bad guys. Getting one or two alive would have been better, but that hadn't happened.

The bad news was that Ellis Starkey and Tommy Grotto, along with a third guy by the name of Waylon Brooks, were still in the wind.

And those were only the guys they knew about. He and the rest of the tactical team suspected there were others too.

Having illegal guns flooding the streets had led to dozens of shooting incidents, with more on the horizon. As if being a member of the tactical team wasn't dangerous enough. They were being called to participate in more takedowns and tactical situations than ever before.

"Ms. Crane," he began.

"Please call me Harper," she interrupted. "Ma'am makes me feel old. And I'm not accustomed to people calling me by my maiden name." She shook her head. "I was such a fool. I thought Jake was perfect for me, that we'd be married for decades the way my parents were. But I couldn't have been more wrong."

"I'm sorry, Harper." Using her given name made it difficult to remain professional. "But keep in mind, Jake created an illusion. You couldn't have known the truth he kept hidden for so long."

"I won't make that mistake again," she murmured. Then she sighed. "I wish there was more I could tell you. Truly. But I swear I don't know anything."

He believed her, yet that meant there was likely only one reason they'd attempted to kidnap her. And that was to force Jake into not testifying. Someone within the gun-running organization must have realized he wasn't dead.

He had to keep that thought to himself, though, as he wasn't cleared to share any details of their investigation with her.

"Okay, there's one last thing we need from you." He rose to his feet. "I'm going gather several mug shots for you to look at. I need you to tell me if any of the men look familiar."

"I can do that." She hesitated, then said, "Thank you, Officer Delany. I appreciate your kindness."

"You may as well call me Steele," he said, turning toward the door. "I'll be back in a few minutes."

As he stepped outside the interview room, he found Joe Kingsley and Brock Greer standing there.

"You sure she's not hiding anything?" Joe asked.

He could tell Brock had given Joe an earful. "Anything is possible, but I find it difficult to believe she'd hold back from us knowing her baby is at risk. She doesn't have any love for her ex-husband either."

Joe nodded thoughtfully. "Yeah, I heard enough to agree with you. Brock, as you know, still has his doubts. Pull together those mug shots and see if she can identify anyone."

"Sure thing." He knew Brock had trust issues from events in his personal life, so Steele let it go. For his part, he couldn't help but feel bad about her situation. Maybe because he was still grieving the loss of his girlfriend, Monique.

He found Raelyn putting the mug shots together for him on the computer. It was easier and faster than using paper or lineups.

"I heard the perps got away," she said without looking at him. "I have Gabe Melrose our tech guy searching street camera footage for the vehicle."

"Thanks." He appreciated Rae's chipping in to help. Despite being a talented cop, she was always willing to offer her assistance in any way.

Jina, on the other hand, balked at doing what she called scut work. Unless, of course, Joe or Rhy personally assigned tasks to her. He didn't mind working with the handful of female cops on their team, but Jina had a chip on her shoulder the size of Everest.

He grabbed the closest laptop and booted it up. Within

five minutes, Rae had sent him the six-packs she'd put together. He brought each of the three groupings up on the screen, then minimized two of them.

Carrying the laptop to the interview room, he placed it in front of Harper. She looked surprised, then leaned forward with interest to study the first group of six men.

She took her time, studying each face for a long moment before moving on. But at the end, she sat back. "I'm sorry. None of these guys look familiar."

"That's okay, let's try the next one." He hadn't expected her to identify Tommy Grotto, the guy was a chameleon, blending into his surroundings. He brought up the next group of six faces.

"That's Ellis Starkey." She pointed at the face in the middle of the bottom row. "I guess I didn't realize he'd been arrested."

"He hasn't, we just happened to get a good picture of him." He minimized that screen and brought up the last six pictures.

She studied them again, then shook her head. "Nope. Never saw any of these guys before."

He shouldn't be surprised that she hadn't been able to identify Waylon Brooks. He glanced up at the one-way glass and gave a small shrug.

Disappointed that they hadn't learned much from this interview, he closed the laptop. "Okay, thanks for your help."

"Does this mean I can go back to work?" She looked surprised and a bit apprehensive.

He hesitated. Joe hadn't mentioned getting approval for a safe house for her. "Yes. I'll drive you back to the law offices. However, you really shouldn't go anywhere alone." Team members would continue keeping an eye on her, but that wasn't foolproof. If they'd been a few yards farther back, they may not have been able to rescue her in time.

"Okay." She stood and reached for her coat. He found himself holding it for her so she could slip her arms in the sleeves. "Thanks."

"You're welcome." He cleared his throat, reminding himself that she was a victim of a crime, not a potential date. And pregnant to boot. He wasn't interested in going down the relationship path again. gave himself a mental shake as he opened the door for her, glad to see both Joe and Brock weren't still hanging around.

"This way." He still had the keys to the squad, so he didn't bother to find Brock. It didn't sit well with him to drop Harper off at the law offices, but he escorted her outside anyway.

She didn't say anything until he pulled up to the skyscraper housing the prestigious law offices of the Gibson and Roberts. Ironically, their specialty was criminal defense. They made their money defending people like her ex-husband. "Off—er—Steele, will I be safe going home tonight?"

"Do you have friends or family you can stay with?"

"Not really. My parents passed away last year." She grimaced and reached for her door handle. "Never mind. I'm sure I'll be fine."

"Hold on." He slipped out from behind the wheel, raking his gaze over the area as he went around the back to her side. He opened her door for her. "I'll walk you inside."

As she emerged from the squad, the sound of gunfire reverberated around them.

"Get in! Keep your head down!" He shoved her back down inside the squad and used his radio to call for backup. When another bullet shattered the windshield, he hunkered down behind the vehicle, trying to pinpoint the location of the shooter.

The answer to her question was a big fat no. Harper Crane was far from safe. And he still wasn't sure why she'd been targeted.